The Animals' Bedtime Storybook

To Liam, Hannah, Ryan and Warren
from G.A. Wendy

To the Hayes family
with love P.D.

First published in Great Britain in 2000
by Orion Children's Books
a division of the Orion Publishing Group Ltd
Orion House
5 Upper Saint Martin's Lane
London WC2H 9EA

Compilation © Wendy Cooling 2000
Illustrations © Penny Dann 2000
All stories remain the copyright © of the
individual authors, listed on the contents page iv

Designed by Tracey Cunnell

The moral right of Wendy Cooling, Lucy Coats,
Alan Durant, Vivian French, Adèle Geras, Michael Lawrence,
Jenny Nimmo, Jeremy Strong, Jean Ure and Penny Dann to be
identified as the authors and illustrator of this work has been asserted.

A catalogue record for this book is available from the British Library

Printed in Italy by Printer Trento S.r.l.

The Animals' Bedtime Storybook

Compiled by Wendy Cooling
Illustrated by Penny Dann

Orion
Children's Books

Contents

The Animals on the Ark   7

Day 1 - The Beaver's Story   Jenny Nimmo   11

Day 2 - The Hippopotamus's Story   Jean Ure   21

Day 3 - The Crocodile's Story   Vivian French   27

Day 4 - The Leopard's Story   Adèle Geras   33

Day 5 - The Mongoose's Story   Jenny Nimmo   38

Day 6 - The Dog's Story   Lucy Coats   43

Day 7 - The Cow's Tale   Alan Durant   49

Day 8 - King Cobra's Story   Jenny Nimmo   57

Day 9 - The Ocelot's Tale   Jeremy Strong   59

Day 10 - The Porcupine's Story   Michael Lawrence   65

Day 11 - The Bee and the Wasp's Story   Vivian French   70

Day 12 - The Wolf's Story   Michael Lawrence   73

Day 13 - The Moth's Story   Adèle Geras   81

Day 14 - The Elephant's Story   Jean Ure   84

Day 15 - The Cat's Story   Michael Lawrence   92

Day 16 - The Hamster's Story   Jeremy Strong   96

Day 17 - The Lioness's Story   Jenny Nimmo   99

Day 18 - The Giraffe's Story   Adèle Geras   104

Day 19 - The Sparrow's Story   Alan Durant   106

Day 20 - The Stick Insect's Story   Jeremy Strong   110

Day 21 - The Chameleon's Story   Jeremy Strong   112

Day 22 - The Bear's Story   Lucy Coats   119

Day 23 - The Rabbit's Story   Adèle Geras   126

Day 24 - The Camel's Story   Vivian French   131

Day 24 - The Kingfisher's Story   Lucy Coats   140

Day 26 - The Guinea Pig's Story   Jean Ure   148

Day 27 - The Skunk's Story   Michael Lawrence   152

Day 28 - The Jackdaw's Story   Jenny Nimmo   155

Day 29 - The Tortoise's Story   Vivian French   160

Day 30 - The Tiger's Story   Jean Ure   165

Day 31 - The Slug's Story   Michael Lawrence   170

Day 32 - The Pig's Story   Lucy Coats   175

Day 33 - The Warthog's Story   Jeremy Strong   178

Day 34 - The Bobcat's Story   Alan Durant   182

Day 35 - The Penguin's Story   Alan Durant   188

Day 36 - The Worm's Story   Jean Ure   194

Day 37 - The Parrot's Story   Vivian French   198

Day 38 - The Duck's Story   Adèle Geras   204

Day 39 - The Owl's Story   Lucy Coats   211

Day 40 - The Lovebird's Story   Alan Durant   217

Did You See?   224

The People who Wrote the Stories

LUCY COATS: The very first book I ever wrote for children, called *One Hungry Baby*, was full of baby animals. When I was a little girl, I had a pet bantam called Rowena, who always sat on the back of my car seat on the way to school. My Number One favourite animal is definitely a bear, although when I came face to face with a big Brown Bear on a recent visit to America, I ran away! I live with two mad dogs who look like long electrocuted perms with bottlebrush tails. They leap at flies all day, and always look surprised when they miss.

ALAN DURANT: I live with a feisty aged cat called Puddy, who appears in my book *Jake's Magic*. I've written lots of books featuring animals, including *Snake Supper*, *Big Fish Little Fish* and *Mouse Party*. In my *Spider McDrew* stories, the main character has a pet cow, and the star of my recent book *Creepe Hall for Ever!* is a six-legged mechanical cat called Tiddles!

VIVIAN FRENCH: I love animals. They don't worry about whether they're fat, or whether they've got their fur nicely brushed. They just get on with their lives, eating, sleeping – or watching me watching them! I've written about all kinds of animals – frogs in *Growing Frogs*, spiders in *Spider Watching*, whales in *Whale Journey* – and wolves and foxes and bears and all sorts in *Aesop's Funky Fables*. My favourite? Morris – the cat in *Morris and the Cat Flap*.

ADÈLE GERAS: I'm fond of the animals whose tales I tell in this book. I love giraffes best because I used to see them when I lived in Africa, a long time ago. But my very favourite creature of all is the cat. We have a lovely cat called Mimi and I'm devoted to her. I've written a series of four stories written in cats' voices, called *The Cats of Cuckoo Square*.

MICHAEL LAWRENCE: I once worked for a travelling circus. It was part of my job to buy sheeps' heads to feed to the lions and tigers. I didn't like this job much and have never written a story about it. I've written lots of other stories, though. Books too. One of the books is called *The Poppykettle Papers*. Another is called *The Killer Underpants*. Neither of them has anything to do with sheep.

JENNY NIMMO: I've always had at least one animal in my life. As a child I wasn't much interested in dolls or stuffed toys. Animals were my preferred friends. Last year I reared a baby jackdaw, and when it had learned to fly, it would dive out of the sky and land on my head. An astonishing and wonderful sensation.

JEREMY STRONG: Animals have always been BIG in my life. My first favourite book, when I was four, was called *Winky the Squirrel*. We have always had pet cats, but also a dog, hamsters, gerbils, mice, goldfish and stick insects. I would love a pet tiger, but my wife won't let me. She says our cat flap isn't big enough.

Some of my stories with animals: *The Hundred Mile an Hour Dog*, *My Dad's Got an Alligator!*, *Dinosaur Pox*, *Problems with a Python*, *Max and the Petnappers*.

JEAN URE: I have been making up stories ever since I can remember – my very first book was published while I was still at school, and writing is the only real job I have ever had. As well as making up stories I help look after our family of seven rescued dogs and four rescued cats. This is why I have written lots of books about animals!

If you enjoy reading about animals, try *the puppy present*.

The Animals on the Ark

It was pouring with rain. Water covered the whole earth. Noah had built an Ark to keep the animals safe and dry – just two of every kind, because the Ark wasn't big enough for them all.

Noah had been working for weeks to build the Ark – chopping down trees, sawing logs, hammering, nailing and glueing.

At last it was ready, and today Noah stood on the deck counting the animals on to the Ark, two by two by two.

There were . . .

penguins

pandas

worms

guinea pigs

zebras

hippos

elephants

sheep

crocodiles

8

leopards

bears

monkeys

giraffes

snakes

hyenas

buffaloes

squirrels

and lots, lots more.

There were two of every kind and there were so many that Noah soon lost count!

Can you help him put them together into pairs?

How many different animals can you see in the picture?

How many more animals can you think of?

But at last all the animals were safely on board. Noah gave them their supper.

"Time for bed, everyone!" said Noah. "Find somewhere to settle down, and we'll all have a good night's sleep."

But not all the animals wanted to go to sleep. Some of them – like the owls and the bats – were wide awake. The monkeys chattered, the dogs barked, the geese honked, the hyenas howled. It was not peaceful.

"I can't sleep!" said a warthog crossly. "The donkeys keep braying."

"I don't like it here," squeaked a tiny vole. "There's an eagle looking at me."

"The rain's keeping me awake," said a camel.

"None of us will ever get a wink of sleep here," grumbled a big brown bear.

"Stop it!" shouted Noah. "You animals don't know how lucky you are. I've been working for weeks to make sure you're safe, and all you can do is complain. Just go to sleep!"

"But we can't sleep with all this racket," said a grumpy gorilla.

"Why don't you tell us a story, Noah?" asked a kangaroo. "My mother always used to tell me stories to send me to sleep."

"Good idea!" said a porcupine, and the toucans nodded their heads.

"All right," said Noah. "I'll tell you a story. But you must all be very quiet."

The animals squeaked and squawked and shuffled and shushed. At last they were all settled. Noah sat in the middle of a big circle with Mrs Noah and their sons, Shem, Ham and Japhet.

"Can you all hear me?" asked Noah. "Then I'll begin."

The Beaver's Story

Jenny Nimmo

"This is a story," said Noah, "about –" he looked round at all the animals – "about two beavers."

The beavers looked pleased.

"Who wants to hear a story about beavers? Why not ocelots?" said a handsome ocelot.

"You can have your own story later," said Noah. "In fact, you can all take turns telling stories every night. Now, let me get on with my story."

"When Bakbuk was three weeks old, his mother knew that he would be a famous beaver. His teeth were enormous.

" 'Ouch!' she cried when she suckled him. 'That's enough!'

"She dragged a pile of bark into their lodge and said, 'Now chew on that!'

"Bakbuk went through the pile in minutes.

11

"The beaver family lived in a big lodge made of bark, mud and twigs. Bakbuk had five older brothers and five sisters the same age as he was, so the family needed a lot of room.

"Beavers spend most of their time building dams, long walls of mud, stones and branches. They build their dams across fast-flowing streams and behind the dams the water rises and rises until it forms a wide marshy lake. This is where the beavers build their lodges. The entrance is under water, so the beavers can only get inside by swimming up a tunnel. Beavers are great swimmers. Bakbuk was one of the best.

"As soon as he was old enough, Bakbuk followed his parents across the moonlit lake and watched them felling a tree. When they both worked together they could gnaw through a tree trunk very quickly.

"CRASH! A willow thundered to the ground.

"Bakbuk was impressed. 'I could do that,' he cried.

"'No,' said his father. 'You couldn't do that – yet.'

"'I could! I could!' Bakbuk jumped up and down in his excitement. 'I've got the biggest teeth in the family.'

"'We don't need any trees at the moment, dear,' his mother said gently. 'This one will do very nicely. We'll gnaw it into logs and ferry it across to our larder. The bark will last us for at least a month.'

"'Bark! Bark! Bark!' yelled Bakbuk. 'I adore bark!'

"'Keep your voice down,' said his father. "We don't want the hunters to find us. They'll have our fur in no time.'

"Bakbuk helped his parents to gnaw the big tree into logs, and then push them through long canals to the beaver larder. He felt very pleased with himself.

"'Well done, Bakbuk,' said his father. 'You've been very helpful.'

"'We think you deserve a treat," said his mother. 'What would you like to do tomorrow?'

"'I'd like to gnaw through a tree all by myself,' said Bakbuk.

"'You can't do that,' his father told him. 'We've got enough trees for now. Tell you what, I'll take you swimming. We'll go up-country and I'll show you the snowy mountains.'

"Bakbuk didn't want to see snowy mountains. He wanted to gnaw down a tree. He sulked. His brothers were shocked.

"'We didn't get to see the snowy mountains until we were a whole year old,' said Ben, the biggest brother. 'And here you are, only six months old, sulking. You should be clapping your paws for joy.'

"Bakbuk hung his head.

"'I can't help it,' he said. 'All I want to do is gnaw.'

"'You're spoilt,' said his sisters. 'Dad hasn't asked us along to see the snowy mountains.'

"'You haven't got big teeth,' said Bakbuk.

"That afternoon his parents had a long nap. They were very tired after a whole night of gnawing. Their children fell asleep around them, all except Bakbuk. He lay among his dreaming family, listening to the snores and whimpers, the heavy breathing, and all he could think about was gnawing wood.

"He began to grind his teeth. 'Ngrr-ngrr-ngrr-ngrr.'

"His mother woke up.

"'Ssh! Stop it, Bakbuk!'

"'Sorry,' Bakbuk whispered. 'My teeth ache.'

"'Go to sleep,' said his mother, 'and then you won't notice.' She rolled over and began to snore.

"Bakbuk closed his eyes as tight as he could, but sleep would not come. There was only one thing for it. Slowly, and very quietly, he crawled away from his brothers and sisters and slipped into the watery tunnel that led out of the lodge. He swam through the entrance and then he was in the cool marshy lake.

"'Yippee!' he squeaked, and made for the shore.

"There were so many trees to choose from, Bakbuk didn't know where to start. At last he chose a tall, silvery birch tree. He was just about to bite into it when a voice said, 'That's my tree!'

"Bakbuk looked over his shoulder. There, sitting on a tree-stump, was another beaver. A female.

"'Er, hullo,' said Bakbuk. 'Who are you?'

"'Bathsheba,' said the female. 'And you?'

"'Bakbuk,' said Bakbuk. 'I'm sorry, Bathsheba, but this tree is much too big for you.'

"'Huh!' said Bathsheba. 'I'll show you! Stand back!'

"Bakbuk was so surprised he did stand back. Bathsheba leapt down, ran to the tree and gnawed through the trunk in ten minutes flat.

"Bakbuk was amazed.

"'Your teeth must be as big as mine,' he said.

"'Let's have a competition,' Bathsheba suggested.

"'You're on,' said Bakbuk.

"The willow Bakbuk chose crashed to the ground at exactly the same time as Bathsheba's alder. They rushed on to the next two trees. Bakbuk had never enjoyed himself so much.

"'This is the best day of my life,' he muttered through a mouthful of splinters.

"'Mine too,' mumbled Bathsheba.

"After an hour their teeth began to ache, so they stopped gnawing for a moment and looked around. What they saw scared them, just a bit. Eight big trees lay in a rough circle all around the two beavers.

"'Oh dear,' said Bakbuk. 'My dad's not going to like this.'

"'I'm going home,' said Bathsheba.

"Bakbuk was right. His father didn't like what he had just done, one little bit.

"'You can't go gnawing down trees just for fun,' he ranted. 'It's not allowed. The beaver elders will make you leave the forest. Tree-felling is serious business. You must learn to control your life, Bakbuk. I forbid you to leave the lodge for a week.'

"'No snowy mountains for you,' Ben muttered with a smirk.

"Poor Bakbuk. Staying indoors was agony. He told himself all sorts of stories to take his mind off gnawing, but somehow a tree always popped into the story. Bakbuk's teeth seemed to have a life of their own and he knew that if he didn't get into the forest very soon, he would gnaw off his foot or Ben's tail. Ben wouldn't stop teasing him.

"There was only one thing Bakbuk could do. Escape. So one warm afternoon, when the family were asleep, Bakbuk slid into the watery tunnel and swam across the lake.

"It felt so good to be out. Bakbuk did a little dance before choosing his tree. As he bounced about, he saw, out of the corner of his eye, another beaver doing the same thing.

They both stopped dancing. The other beaver was Bathsheba.

"'Hullo!' they both said. 'What are you doing here?'

"Bakbuk told Bathsheba what had happened to him. She told him the same story. She even had a sister who kept teasing her.

"'I thought I'd just have a quick nibble and then slip back before anyone noticed I had gone,' said Bakbuk.

"'Me too,' said Bathsheba. 'Let's nibble the same tree.'

"They nibbled an alder. Bathsheba on one side, Bakbuk on the other. they nibbled and nibbled. They gnawed and gnawed, and before they knew it the tree had fallen. Crash!

"But one tree wasn't enough. In no time at all twelve trees had crashed to the ground.

"'Oh dear,' said Bakbuk. 'I hope the beaver elders don't get to hear about this.'

"'I'm going home,' said Bathsheba.

"The falling trees had made such a din, the beaver elders could hardly help hearing about it. That night they held a council. Bakbuk and Bathsheba were told to attend. A great many speeches were made. Bakbuk's mother wept and pleaded, but it was no use. The beaver elders had made up their minds. Bakbuk and Bathsheba would have to leave.

"'It's them or us,' said the oldest beaver. 'Soon there'll be no trees left in the forest.'

"Below them the wild river tumbled into a shining lake.

"'I'm sorry it had to be this way,' said the oldest beaver. 'But it's a big world. You'll soon find another forest. Good luck!'

"'One day you'll be famous,' wept Bakbuk's mother. 'You're such a special beaver.'

"The four beaver parents kissed their children goodbye, and then Bakbuk and Bathsheba were alone. They looked out at the great moonlit lake. It seemed to have no end.

"'It *is* a big world,' sighed Bakbuk.

"'Maybe someone out there needs us,' murmured Bathsheba.

"'Someone who wants a lot of wood,' said Bakbuk.

"'To build an enormous lodge,' said Bakbuk.

"'Yesss!' cried both the beavers, and together they jumped into the shining water."

The Hippopotamus's Story

Jean Ure

"Now, who wants to take a turn telling a story?" said Noah as all the animals settled down the next night. "How about you hippos? Do you know any good stories?"

"Good stories? I should say so!" said one great big hippopotamus.

"I will tell you my very favourite story," said the other great big hippopotamus. "Come close, everyone, and listen carefully." And so she began.

"Once upon a time, there was a little hippo called Hatty who longed to be a dancer."

"What sort of dancer?" one of the hyenas wanted to know.

"Well … a ballet dancer."

"A *ballet* dancer? Pardon me while I laugh!" said the hyena. And he opened his mouth and went, "Hohohoheeeeeeeeeha!"

The two little guinea pigs giggled. An elephant smiled. Even a sleeping sloth woke up and grinned.

But the hyena! He was doubled over.

"Oh, he e e e e e e e e hohohe e e e e e e hahe e e ! A ballet dancer!"

"Yes," said the hippo. "That's just what her family said. A *ballet* dancer. Ho ho ho! they went. Ha ha ha! They laughed and they laughed. It was just so funny… Hatty the Huge, wanting to be a ballerina!"

"Well, really, I ask you," said the hyena, wiping his eyes on the back of his paw.

"I suppose it must seem rather ridiculous," agreed the hippo. "Hatty's mum did her best to talk her out of it. 'Hippos aren't dancers,' she said. 'We're **clumpers**, not dancers.'

"And she went clumping off along the river bank. **Clump clump, clumpity clump**.

"And Hatty's brother and sister went with her. **Clump clump, clumpity clump**.

"And all her aunties and uncles and cousins went **clumping** after.

"Hatty's dad said, 'Cheer up, lass! There's plenty of other things for a hippo to do.'

"But Hatty didn't want to do other things! She wanted to be a dancer.

"She wandered off along the river, trying very hard not to **clump**, until she came to the Splashy Pool, where the swans hung out.

"Hatty loved to watch the swans! They had such long, elegant necks (Hatty's neck was short and thick) and they looked so graceful as they glided across the pool.

"When Hatty went into the water she did it with a great SPLOSH! She created tidal waves. The swans hardly even made a ripple!

"Hatty stood watching as they danced their water ballet, *Swan Lake*. How she longed to be as sleek and slender as a swan!

"That was the moment she made up her mind: she was going to be the world's first hippo ballerina!

23

"Her family couldn't think what had come over her.

"Her sister would say, 'Let's go off eating! I know where there's some scrummy new plants!'

"But Hatty would shake her head and say, 'You go. I'm not hungry.'

"Even when they visited McHippo's for an evening meal, Hatty would only nibble at a few fronds of water weed (making sure it wasn't the fattening sort).

"Very soon, Hatty was one slim hippo! Her neck was still short, but at least it wasn't *thick*; and she could wave her legs in the air really beautifully!

"Hatty's mum was worried.

"'This is not natural,' she said. 'A hippo should be fat, not thin!'

"But Hatty just grew thinner and thinner. Now that she had started, she found it difficult to stop.

"One day she discovered she was so slender she could slide into the water without making any ripples, just like the swans!

"She invented her own water ballet, *Hippo Lake*, in which she danced the part of a beautiful young maiden who had been turned by an evil magician into a hippopotamus. Animals came from far and wide to watch her dance. She was the very first hippo ballerina!

"But the other hippos shook their heads and said, 'Why does she think it's so bad to be a hippopotamus? We're *proud* to be hippopotamuses! We *like* being big and fat! That is the way hippopotamuses are supposed to be!'

"But Hatty just grew thinner and thinner. And th..i..n..n..e..r and th...i...n...n...e...r and th....i....n....n....e....r.... Until one day she found that she didn't have the strength to do her water ballet any more. She sank down on to the sandy bank by the side of the river and thought, 'Oh, dear! I feel so weak.'

"If a hungry lion had come along –" The hippopotamus paused.

"What, what?" squeaked the guinea pigs.

"He would have gobbled her up!"

"Eeeeegh!" The guinea pigs gave little squeals of horror.

"If a hungry hyena had come along," said the hyena, "he would have gobbled her up!"

"Hush," said the elephant. "You're frightening the little ones!"

But the hyena only showed his teeth and went, "Teeeheee!"

"So what happened?" said the sloth, opening one eye.

"Oh! Well," said the hippopotamus. "I gave up being a ballerina and went back to being a hippo. It's far more fun!"

"Fat and happy," murmured the hyena. "You'd make a good meal, now!"

"Ah, but only if you could catch me," said Hatty. "Which you couldn't, because I should create a tidal wave and drown you!"

One of the guinea pigs was tugging at the elephant's trunk.

"What dear?" said the elephant.

"Was she Hatty all along?" whispered the guinea pig.

"Yes," beamed the elephant. "Hatty the happy hippo. Wasn't that a lovely story?"

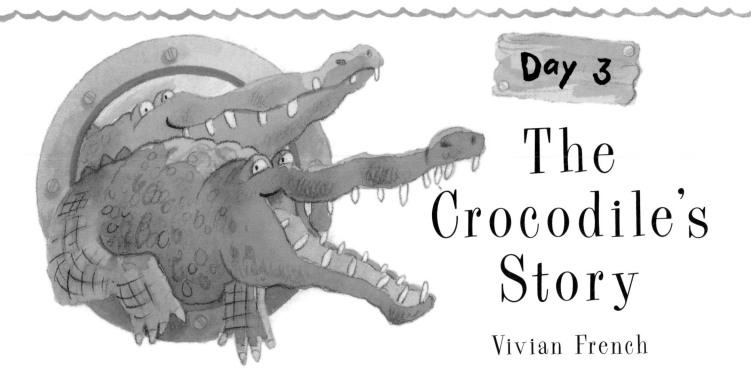

The Crocodile's Story

Vivian French

The two crocodiles were lying very still. Very still indeed. So still that the monkeys had quite forgotten they were there.

"Ha ha ha! Hee hee hee! We can climb to the top of a tree!" the monkeys sang. And they danced nearer and nearer to the crocodiles until suddenly –

"CROCODILES!" shouted Noah.

Both the crocodiles closed their wide open mouths with an angry snap. The monkeys leapt into Mrs Noah's lap where they hugged each other and chattered loudly.

"There will be NO eating other animals on this ark!" Noah said. "I've told you before and I'm telling you now!"

The two crocodiles looked at each other. You couldn't be sure, but maybe one of them winked.

"My dear Mr Noah," said the biggest, oldest crocodile. "I wouldn't DREAM of eating any of your little friends. I was just – yawning. You see, I'm afraid I didn't care for their singing."

He shook his huge scaly head from side to side, and sighed. "I'm a singer myself, you see."

"A singer? *You?*" A monkey, safe on Mrs Noah's knee, pulled a face. "Crocodiles can't sing!"

The crocodile heaved another heavy sigh.

"But I can, young monkey, I can. It's just that I don't, and I don't because I have promised not to."

The crocodile smiled a small sad smile, and two large tears trickled down his leathery cheeks.

"Perhaps I should tell you my story."

"Please do," said Noah, and the monkeys nodded.

All the other animals came a little closer, and the crocodile's smile grew just a little wider.

"So kind," he said. "So very kind. Now, let me begin at the beginning.

I have always sung. I was born with the most beautiful voice in the whole wide world; everyone said so. Even when I was a mere egg I sang, and the other eggs would roll themselves nearer to hear me. When I was a hatchling and took my first swim in the river the hippopotamuses cheered and cheered until my mother took me away for my midday nap. The lions and the tigers and the camels and the water buffalo travelled for miles to hear me, and the nightingales came to ask me to sing at their night time concerts.

When I sang the trees never rustled, the streams never babbled and the river never splashed … the whole world was still and silent as my voice swooped and soared."

The crocodile stopped for a moment, and another two large tears rolled slowly down his nose.

"What happened?" whispered a tiny rabbit.

"Alas, alack … oh woe is me," said the crocodile. "I can hardly bear to tell you …" and his husky, dusty voice was very faint.

The animals edged closer.

"PLEASE tell us," said the tiny rabbit. "PLEASE!"

The crocodile nodded.

"Very well, my dear little rabbit … but forgive me if it is hard for me … forgive me if I speak so that some of you cannot hear … some of you are rather far away …"

The listening animals silently edged nearer and nearer.

"It all ended," the crocodile went on, "on a clear and moonlit night. I had been singing for many, many hours, and my sweet, kind, loving mama came to tell me that I would wear my voice away. I said I would sing one last song, and then I would come home.

"'Be sure you do, my lovely one,' said my mama, and she went back to make my night time drink.

I sang my song and said goodnight to my wonderful audience. They cheered and clapped for many minutes. Then … oh me. Alas and oh my … Oh, the memory!"

The crocodile covered his eyes for a long long moment.

"I was walking slowly and wearily towards my river bed when I heard it. A terrible, TERRIBLE noise … the most dreadful noise I have ever, ever heard …"

The crocodile stopped again, and sobbed loudly.

"What was it?" squeaked the tiny rabbit. "PLEASE, Mr Crocodile – what was it?"

"I had sung too long," said the crocodile very, very quietly. "I had sung too long. While they were listening to me the lions and the tigers and the camels and the water buffalo forgot that they were hungry and thirsty. They forgot that they had travelled for many miles with no water or meat … but when I stopped – oh woe, woe, WOE!"

"But I don't understand," said the tiny rabbit. "What did they do?"

The crocodile's voice turned into a feeble croak. "They … they ATE each other, my sweet bunny. And THAT is why I have promised never, NEVER to sing again …"

"OH." The tiny bunny's eyes were very wide. "Oh, Mr Crocodile! How SPLENDID of you! But … have you never sung again?"

"No no no …" said the crocodile. "But I believe that if anyone very VERY small tiptoed into my mouth and listened VERY carefully they might hear a whisper of music … just a whisper …"

"Oh, PLEASE can I try?" The tiny bunny hopped forward, and the crocodile opened his huge sharp-toothed mouth wide …

wider …

WIDER …

"CROCODILE!!"

shouted Noah.

The Leopard's Story

Adèle Geras

"Your turn tonight, Leopard," said Noah. "But please make it a peaceful story, not like Crocodile's. I'm dog-tired!"

The leopard gave a long, lazy yawn, stretched his legs and looked around at the animals, all gathered round him waiting.

"All of you can count yourselves lucky that I'm a nocturnal creature. Do you know what 'nocturnal' means? It means that while most other animals and birds are fast asleep, I am awake and hunting: prowling through the shadows between the trees, guided by the silver light of the moon, and the golden light of the stars. Everything looks different at night. Moving about in the darkness means you have to be very quiet. It would never do to wake my friends, and anyway, padding about on silent paws is a great thing when you're looking out for something to pounce on."

"Oooh," gasped the two little guinea pigs, and shrank in closer to the elephant.

"I haven't always been nocturnal," continued Leopard. "Once, long ago, I slept at night, just like all my other friends in the jungle.

"Sleeping, however, was not the only thing I did. I snored. Have you ever heard a really loud and noisy snore? My snores were heard for miles around. I made a sound as loud as the waterfall which thundered in the depths of the jungle. The earth trembled and the leaves shook when I breathed in and out. All my closest friends were in despair.

"'We can't get a wink of sleep,' Mama Elephant said to me one day. 'You know that I have six little elephants to look after, and I can tell you we are quite crotchety and cross with one another every day, simply because our sleep has been disturbed. It's a well-known fact. All creatures, whatever their size, need a good night's sleep for the sake of their health and happiness.'

"'I *do* know,' I said, 'and I'm sorry, I really am. But what can I do about it?'

"'Have you tried sleeping on your back?'

"'With all four paws sticking up into the air, you mean? Oh, I couldn't do that! That's a most uncomfortable position for any cat, big or small.'

"Mama Elephant sighed and went back to her children.

So it went on, night after night. All the animals came to me with suggestions about how I could stop snoring, but nothing worked. I snored as loudly as ever.

"Then, one day, a humming-bird came fluttering into the jungle and said to me:

"'I can cure you of your snoring, but it will mean changing your habits forever. Do you mind?'

"'That depends,' I answered. 'What sort of changes do you mean?'

"'Well, I'm going to stop you snoring by stopping you from sleeping.'

"'You can't do that!' I said. 'Mama Elephant says we all need to sleep for our health and happiness.'

"'That's quite true,' hummed the little bird, 'but sleeping is just as good for you whenever you do it. What I meant was: I would stop you sleeping at night, and then you'd have to sleep during the day. How about that?'

"'We could try it, I suppose,' I said. I was desperate by this time.

"The next night, just as I was settling down on my favourite branch, the little humming-bird popped its head out of the leaves and said:

"'Here I am. Are you ready?'

"'I'm always ready for sleep. I'm a very good sleeper indeed.'

"'Goodnight, then.'

"'What do I have to do?'

"'Go to sleep and start snoring.'

"So that is what I did, and every single time the humming-bird heard even the first hint of a snore, he came straight down and began to hum loudly in my ear. Of course I woke up at once. I fell asleep and woke up hundreds of times in the night, but the silence that spread in the jungle while that little bird tormented me was beautiful.

"Next day, everyone was in a very good mood except me, I was completely exhausted. As the sun rose in the sky, I found a shady branch, and climbed on it and fell into a deep and dream-filled slumber. By the time the sun went down, I'd been asleep for hours, so there was nothing to do but prowl through the darkness.

"I fell in love with the night, as I walked in the moonlight. While everyone else was lost in their dreams, I padded silently through the undergrowth on my velvet paws. The air was cool and pleasant, and the silence soothed me and made me feel peaceful and calm. By the time the daylight came round again, my wanderings had quite tired me out, and I found another branch to lie on all day.

"And so it has continued. I walk about in the night time, and I sleep during the day. I snore during the day too, sometimes, but of course the other birds and animals are chattering and squawking so much that no one pays me any attention at all. And now, I am wide awake to tell this story. Tomorrow, when most of you stroll around the deck of this little ark, I shall find a corner somewhere and curl up quietly … or maybe not so quietly. If you listen very carefully, you will probably hear me snoring. And you'll remember the little humming-bird who taught me how to be nocturnal."

The Mongoose's Story

Jenny Nimmo

"Who's going to tell us a story tonight?" said Noah. "A giraffe? A rat? A tiger?"

"I know a story," said a mongoose. "It's a very exciting one. I was very brave."

"Were you indeed," said Noah. "Why don't you tell us about it?"

So the mongoose began.

"I miss the family I lived with. There was a boy, two girls and a baby. They all loved me.

"The boy was naughty. If it hadn't been for him I'd still be there, living in a cool house with tasty insects in the kitchen, and rats under the verandah. I like eating rats – and scorpions, and even fat snakes. That's why the family loved me. I ate the things they were afraid of.

"The boy just wouldn't do as he was told.

"'Don't climb on the roof,' said the father. The boy climbed on the roof and fell off.

"'Don't swim in the river,' said the mother. The boy swam in the river and nearly got eaten by a crocodile.

"'Don't go near the jungle,' said the grandmother. The boy went into the jungle, was bitten by a snake and nearly died.

"That's where I came in.

"It was one of those really steamy afternoons. I was so hot I didn't want to move. I just wanted to snooze on the cool verandah. The children were all asleep, or should have been. It was so quiet you could have heard a scorpion think.

"There was a soft thump from the back of the house. I knew that sound. The boy had jumped out of the window. He's done it before.

"I ran to the verandah steps just in time to see him streaking past and onto the path that led beside the Wallawalla river.

"'Wait!' I squeaked.

"The boy took no notice, of course. What could I do? I had to follow him, in case something nasty happened, which it did, of course."

"What happened, what happened?" the monkeys chattered in unison.

"All in good time, my friends," replied the mongoose.

"The boy ran very fast for a human. Before I could catch up with him there was a terrible scream. And there it was: a huge King Cobra. It had reared up so that it was as tall as the boy; taller in fact.

"Ooooh," twittered the monkeys, hugging each other.

"King Cobras are the worst creatures in the world," the mongoose continued. "One bite from their poisonous fangs and you've only got a few minutes to live."

"Now, look here …" protested Cobra.

But the mongoose kept right on with his story.

"I didn't hesitate. I flew at that hideous, hissing snake-head and bit into the scary hood behind its neck. The snake was furious. It raged and screamed. It shook me against a tree-trunk and banged me to the ground. It lashed me with its tail, dragged me through the undergrowth and tried to squash me. But I wouldn't let go, and it couldn't reach me with its deadly fangs."

"That's not right!" said the cobra indignantly.

"Be *quiet,* Cobra," Noah shouted. "Let the mongoose tell his story."

"The boy was very brave. He didn't run away. He just stood there cheering me on.

"'Go on, Manny!' he shouted. 'Brave Manny! Manny the hero!'

"I was feeling so pleased with myself I relaxed my mouth a little and before I knew it, the cobra had slipped into the Wallawalla river.

"'Coward!' I shouted. 'Come back and fight!'

"Big as he was, he was scared of me. He swam out into the middle of the river where I couldn't reach him. I ran along the bank, keeping him in sight. Sometimes I saw his shiny head, sometimes it disappeared. I ran all day and all night. I watched the river until my head swam and I couldn't tell the difference between water and leaves, rocks and snakes. It was all rippling and shining and twinkling and rustling.

"I left my family far behind. I left the boy, the two girls and the baby. I couldn't think of anything but that snake.

"Eventually I realised that I'd lost him. Or had I? I ran beside the river until it became a sea. I ran beside the sea until it became an ocean.

"'He's in there somewhere,' I thought.

"One day I chased a rat on to a wagon and got trapped in a box. We travelled for miles before the driver finally heard my frantic scratching. When he saw that I could kill rats he kept me with him, as a pet. And then he sold me to a woman in a strange, foreign city.

"I lived happily with the woman until the rains came. There was water in the street and water in the house, so I thought I'd better find somewhere safer. That's how I came to be in this creaky old boat. Or is it a house? And he's here too, the King Cobra. He's curled up somewhere in the dark, waiting to strike. I don't trust that King Cobra.

"Don't go near him. Don't even speak to him. He's dangerous. If you do have any trouble with King Cobra, send for me. I'm just about the only creature who can deal with him."

The Dog's Story

Lucy Coats

"It's my turn tonight," hissed the cobra. "The mongoose got that story all wrong. I want to tell my side of it."

"No!" said Noah. "Stop that hissing, and wait your turn like all the others."

"But it's not fair!" said the cobra.

"Calm down," said Noah. "We all want to hear a dog story tonight. Stop lolloping about, you, and let's begin."

The dog gave a big shake and settled down, tucking his tail neatly over his front paws.

"This is an old, old story that my mother told me when I was just a pup.

"Once upon a time there lived a dog King called Fido and his dog Queen, Dido. They lived in the small dog kingdom of Cannis, set between the mountains and the sea, and they were very happy except for one thing – they had no royal puppies. Every night they howled to the Dogstar, Sirius, for help, but no puppies ever came.

"'Maybe Sirius is busy, my dear?' said King Fido, licking his wife's nose comfortingly.

"And it was true, Sirius had millions and millions of dogs to look after. But one night, just as Fido and Dido were starting their evening howl, Sirius happened to look down from the sky and heard their call. Down he swooped and hovered over the palace, twinkling brightly.

"A shower of stardust fell and covered the King and Queen, and sure enough, nine weeks later, seven beautiful puppy princes were born.

"The celebrations went on for days. Every dog in the kingdom was invited, as well as the mountain gnomes and the sea sprites and all the fairydogs, except Fairydog Patchface who was so old and cross that nobody knew (or wanted to know) where she lived.

"Unfortunately, just as the last firework was exploding in the sky, old Fairydog Patchface flew past.

"'A party!' she snarled. 'Why wasn't *I* invited?'

"And down she flapped, down and down into the palace courtyard where the puppies were just receiving gifts from their fairy dogmothers.

"'A curse!' she growled, waving her paw. 'A curse on you all!'

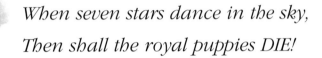

When seven stars dance in the sky,
Then shall the royal puppies DIE!

"And she flew off with a snarl of laughter and was never seen again.

"The King and Queen were in despair, but the smallest fairy dogmother, who had not yet given the puppies her gift, stepped forward.

"'I can't take Patchface's curse away,' she said, 'but I can make it less bad.'

"She took her wand in her teeth and made seven circles around the puppies.

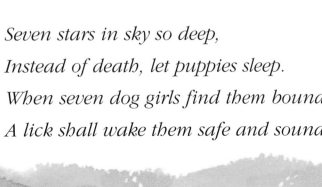
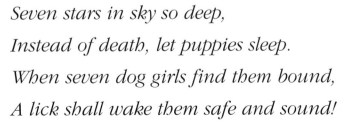

Seven stars in sky so deep,
Instead of death, let puppies sleep.
When seven dog girls find them bound,
A lick shall wake them safe and sound!

"This was all rather mysterious, but the King and Queen were very grateful, and showered the smallest fairydog with presents.

"Next they summoned all the wise old dog astronomers, and asked them to find out when the seven stars would be dancing in the sky. The astronomers looked at their books and charts and shook their ears.

"'We do not know, Your Majesties,' they said. 'And if we do not know then no dog does.'

"So the puppy princes grew up strong and handsome, with straight tails and long drooping ears and shining noses. Their parents were very proud of them, but each night they looked up anxiously at the sky to see if the seven stars were dancing across it yet.

"One spring evening at sunset the princes slipped out of the castle to hunt. They had heard stories of a magical white stag running through the forest, and they wanted to catch it and see if it would grant them each a wish. But as they padded into a clearing in the forest, the moon rose, and when the dog princes looked up at the sky, seven stars circled the moon in a stately dance. At once the princes fell to the ground in a deep sleep, and the young brambles at the edge of the clearing crept round them and over them until they were bound as tight as prisoners.

"King Dido and Queen Fido were frantic when the princes did not appear at supper, and even more frantic when they saw the stars dancing above the castle ramparts. Heralds were sent to each corner of the kingdom and beyond, and a huge reward was offered for the princes' safe return, whether sleeping or waking. But the days and weeks and months went by, and there was no news at all.

"Now it so happened that in the middle of the forest there lived an old dog doctor with his seven beautiful dog daughters. Each day they would set off through the forest to gather herbs and berries and flowers and grasses for their father's potions and lotions.

"One morning in autumn, a herald came by with news of the dog princes' disappearance. The dog girls were very excited, but their father sent them out as usual. So they took their baskets in their mouths and set out to look for blackberries.

"They searched and searched, but there were none to be found in that part of the forest and the dog sisters wandered further and further until suddenly they came to a sunny clearing. There, in front of them, were seven mounds of brambles, covered in the biggest juiciest blackberries they had ever seen. The dog girls picked and picked until their baskets were overflowing, and then they saw … fourteen ears and twenty-eight paws, seven shiny noses, the tips of seven long straight tails.

"The dog sisters ran forward, one to each bramble mound, and scrabbled and scratched and snapped and bit until they could see all seven of the princes lying on the ground. All at once they leant down and gave each prince a lick. The brambles disappeared and the princes sat up, wagging their tails as they opened their eyes and saw the beautiful girls in front of them.

"King Fido and Queen Dido howled with joy as the princes returned, and even Sirius came down to join in with the celebrations, which were the biggest ever seen in the dog kingdom of Cannis. And when the seven happy dog princes married their seven happy dog brides later that day, their wedding cake was filled with big juicy blackberries and even bigger juicy bones."

The Cow's Tale

Alan Durant

"I feel like hearing a funny story tonight," said Noah. "Who can make us laugh? What about one of the cows? I'm sure some funny things have happened to cows."

"Moo! I know a story!" cried the black and white cow. "Let me do it!"

"But it's supposed to be my turn!" said Cobra.

"Your turn will come," said Noah. "Be quiet and listen to the cow's tale."

And the cow began.

"Maisy was a cow, an ordinary, young cow. She lived in a field in a farm. Every day she chewed grass, she swished her tail and she went to the shed to be milked with the other cows. It was not a very exciting sort of life, but it was the only one she knew.

"Then one day everything changed. This is what happened.

"It was a nice spring morning. Maisy was chomping a breakfast of nice, fresh dewy grass and thinking about nothing special. She looked idly up at the sky … Her eyes opened wide. Her mouth froze in mid-chew. This is what she saw.

UNCLE MORT'S RODEO SHOW

See the COWBOY KID in action!
He can lassoo the
WILDEST BEAST!
Come to the show on
Saturday night.
Pond's Field
TICKETS £5 ONLY!

"Maisy stared at the poster of the cowboy and the leaping cow. She stared and she stared and she stared. Then she stared some more and she wondered.

"For the next few days, Maisy watched people come and go in the other field. Big vans and trucks appeared. A huge tent went up. She got more and more excited. Something amazing was going to happen she was sure.

"At last Saturday night came. People flocked into the field. Maisy had never seen such a crowd. They came in cars, they came in coaches, they came in tractors. One man even arrived in a combine harvester. The field was a hum of voices. Into the tent the people went. Then the music started. There was cheering and clapping and yippy-yi-yoing.

"Maisy's tail quivered with excitement.

"'Listen to that!' she said to the other cows. 'What can be going on over there?'

"'Who cares?' said the other cows. 'It's nothing to do with us.'

"'But I want to know what's happening. I want to see,' said Maisy.

"'You're crazy,' said the other cows. 'Eat some grass, go to sleep.'

"But Maisy couldn't go to sleep. She was far too excited. She just had to see what was going on. She had to go over to that other field.

"But how? There was a high hedge all the way around her field and the gate was locked shut. How could Maisy get out?

"Just then Maisy looked up and saw the poster for the rodeo show. She stared at the cowboy and she stared at the leaping cow …

and suddenly she knew what she had to do. Maisy had never jumped before, but now she did not hesitate. She took a few steps back and she charged at the gate."

"Pah!" muttered a horse. "Never heard of a cow that can jump before."

But Cow just glared at Horse and continued with her story.

"High in the air she soared, over the gate, over the road and into the other field.

"She'd made it! Now for the rodeo show.

"The big tent was very noisy. The music was very loud. There was shouting and clapping and stamping. Maisy's ears throbbed and tingled. She found an opening and peeped inside. There was the colourful cowboy, she'd seen him on the poster. He was riding a horse with a rope in his hand, chasing a cow. With a flick of the wrist he threw the rope in the air. It whirred up and forward and around the cow. The cowboy pulled up and the cow fell down.

"'That's no way to treat a cow,' thought Maisy.

"But the crowd were happy. They cheered and whistled and cried for more. The Cowboy Kid raised his hat and bowed. He had a smile as wide as the brim of his hat.

"Suddenly, a hand slapped Maisy on the bottom.

"'Right, on you go,' a rough voice said.

"Maisy was so surprised that she ran forwards. Suddenly, she found herself in the middle of the tent, with lights shining on her and people all around. They were all looking at her.

"'Whoa!' shouted the Cowboy Kid and he started to ride towards Maisy, twirling his rope. Maisy stood and watched him. The Cowboy Kid galloped closer and closer. Whirrrr! The rope flew through the air towards Maisy. The crowd gasped. Maisy jumped. The rope skimmed beneath her and lassoed a fence post.

"The Cowboy Kid fell off his horse and went tumbling down to the ground. His hat rolled in the dust. The crowd 'oohed' then went silent.

"Maisy stood quite still. She looked at the Cowboy Kid and wondered what would happen next. The Cowboy Kid looked very angry. He glared at Maisy, then he picked up his hat and rope and climbed back on his horse. Once more he rode at Maisy with ropes twirling.

"This time, of course, Maisy knew just what to expect. As the rope whirred towards her, she jumped even higher. The rope flew past her and circled a fat man eating an ice-cream. The horse went one way, the Cowboy Kid went the other. He sailed through the air and crashed into a fat man.

"The fat man was actually Uncle Mort. He wasn't happy – and nor was the Cowboy Kid. The ice-cream landed on his head. The Cowboy Kid's hat landed on Uncle Mort. The Cowboy Kid landed on his bottom. The crowd loved it. They laughed and cheered and they stamped their feet.

"Maisy gave a little bow. She was really starting to enjoy herself. This was much more fun than grazing grass or milking.

53

"Now the Cowboy Kid was really mad. He shook his fist at Maisy and said something that sounded like 'Poo!'

"He cleaned the ice-cream off his head, snatched his hat from Uncle Mort, dusted himself down and climbed on the horse once more. He looked mean as a snake – a snake with a bruised bottom.

"Maisy lowed happily. She watched the Cowboy Kid ride away, then turn and gallop towards her.

"'Whoa!' he cried.

"A flick of the wrist and the rope zipped through the air like a bullet. But Maisy was ready. This time she thought she would try something new. She didn't jump. She did a handstand.

"As the rope reached her, she simply flicked it away with her back feet. The rope span for an instant then dropped around the Cowboy Kid as he rode by. Once again the Cowboy Kid fell from his horse and back onto his bottom. His hat flew off. He was tied up like a laced shoe.

"The crowd went wild. Maisy bowed. Then she raised one foot a little and flicked the cowboy's hat up and on to her own head.

"'Bravo!' cried the crowd.

"They stood up and clapped and cheered.

It was the best rodeo they had ever seen.

"'More!' they called. 'More!'

Maisy was only too happy to oblige.

"The Cowboy Kid wasn't finished either. He was furious. No cow was going to make a monkey out of him!

"But Maisy did. Each time the Cowboy Kid tried to catch her, Maisy did some amazing stunt. She jumped and ducked and flipped and dodged and, finally, she did a magnificent backward somersault.

"At last the Cowboy Kid had had enough. He gave up, exhausted.

"The crowd stood up once more. They whistled and cheered and howled with delight. Maisy had to bow and bow and bow.

"'This cow's a star,' said Uncle Mort. 'I must have her in my show.'

"That very night he went to talk to the farmer who owned Maisy.

"So began Maisy's show-business career. She was Maisy, the farm cow, no more. Now she was 'Crazy Maisy', the star of Uncle Mort's Rodeo Show and she was the happiest dang cow in the world! Yes-sirree!

"Yee-haw!"

UNCLE MORT'S RODEO SHOW starring CRAZY MAISY the Wonder Cow!

King Cobra's Story

Jenny Nimmo

"You've got to let me tell my story tonight!" said King Cobra. "It isn't fair. Ever since the mongoose told that terrible story, everybody's been running away from me!"

"Oh, all right, then," said Noah. "Anything for a bit of peace and quiet."

"Now, I'm a King Cobra," said the snake. "I don't eat people. I don't eat big animals. I couldn't swallow them."

King Cobra paused and looked about him.

The two little guinea pigs in the corner squeaked nervously.

"Let me tell you my side of the story," said King Cobra.

"It was a hot afternoon. My wife was sitting on our eggs, thirty-nine of them, to be precise. We'd made a lovely nest in a hollow tree beside the Wallawalla river.

"I must admit I thought the nest was too near a village, but my wife wouldn't have it and I always gave in to her where eggs were concerned.

"I was just gliding away to grab myself a meal (I hadn't eaten for a month) when this boy came tripping along beside the river. Normally I would have ignored him but he was coming rather too close to our nest, so I reared up hissing, just a bit, to scare him off. Goodness! Could that boy scream! The next thing I know, this wretched little mongoose comes bouncing along.

"A mongoose can bite a snake to death, and I didn't want to leave my children fatherless, so I slid into the Wallawalla.

"The mongoose took a bite out of my tail, but I swam into the middle of the river where he couldn't see me. I didn't know the current was so strong. It swept me away from my poor wife and children, and on and on into a great big roaring sea. Someone fished me out. I'm grateful for that. But I wish you wouldn't all treat me as if I were a monster. It's all the mongoose's fault!"

The Ocelot's Tale

Jeremy Strong

"I don't want to hear another peep out of a mongoose or a snake," said Noah. "Let's have a story from – I know, the ocelots. I think you've got a story to tell. Which of you will tell it?"

"I will!" cried one ocelot. It was the male.

"No, let me!" said the other. It was the female. "You always get it wrong."

Noah sighed. "There you go, always bickering. I don't know why you ocelots can't agree with each other. I don't mind who tells the story. Just get on with it."

The male ocelot pushed to the front and sat upright with his neck stretched and his elegant head in the air, so everyone could admire him. The female jostled up next to him. They both began to speak at once.

"When I was still just a cub I had an extraordinary adventure," the male ocelot began.

"My adventure was more extraordinary," said the female ocelot quickly. "In fact it was extra-extra-extra-EXTRAordinary."

59

He tried desperately to ignore her and he went on.

"I was swept away by a river."

"That's nothing," she cried. "I was swept away by a, by a, by a lake!"

The other animals laughed at the quarrelsome pair.

"You are being very stupid," said the male ocelot stiffly. "I was playing beside the river. There had been a tremendous storm in the mountains, and the river was swollen with rainwater. Anyhow, I was pouncing on a small log by the river's edge and suddenly it rolled from beneath me and tumbled into the river, taking me with it. In an instant we were both swept away by the fierce waters. I clung to the log and cried for my mother, but my cries were drowned by the river's roar."

"Rivers can't roar," said she. "Lions roar. Tigers roar. Jaguars and ocelots roar, but rivers just…"

She stopped; she couldn't think what rivers did at all. The male ocelot narrowed his eyes and glared at her.

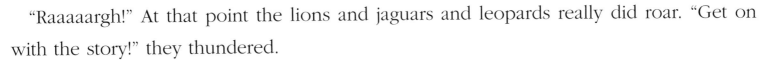

"Yes, what do rivers do?"

"They don't roar," she insisted.

"They just sort of … dribble."

"Dribble! This river was a flood! The waters were churning around so much they uprooted whole trees! Dribble? Huh, that's what you talk, dribble!"

"No I don't!"

"Yes you do!"

"No I don't."

"Yes you …"

"Raaaaargh!" At that point the lions and jaguars and leopards really did roar. "Get on with the story!" they thundered.

The male ocelot settled down.

"I was hurled this way and that by the water. I daren't let go of my log because I was sure I would be drowned."

"I can swim," said the female ocelot proudly. "I would never drown."

"I can swim too," said the male through gritted teeth. "But this happened when I was very small and the current was too strong for me. The river carried me for miles and miles. I was soaked to the bone. I was numb with cold and …"

"I can swim further than you," said the female.

"You don't know that," the male retorted.

"Yes I do. I could swim to China if I wanted to."

"Then why don't you?" he hissed.

"Because I don't want to, so there."

61

The male ocelot turned his back on the female.

"At last I was washed up on a tiny pebble beach, far from home. I could hardly move, except to shiver. My body felt as if it had been battered and bruised all over. At length I managed to stagger to my feet …"

"I can swim underwater too," boasted the female. "I can hold my breath for ages."

A cunning look came into the male ocelot's eyes and he turned back to her.

"Why don't you show everyone how long you can hold your breath for?"

So she did, and while the female held her breath, the male got on with his story.

"I cried for my mother, but of course by this time she was miles away, upriver somewhere. I didn't know what to do. I was cold and I was hungry. It was getting dark. I was scared."

The female ocelot's cheeks were bulging with the enormous breath she was still holding in. She had gone cross-eyed with the effort. The male ocelot smiled secretly and carried on.

"Then there was a great beating of wings and an enormous bird flapped down beside me. It was a condor. He eyed me this way and that way. I got ready to fight. I knew he would try and eat me, and he looked pretty hungry to me. Of course, a condor is no threat to me now that I am fully grown, but I was small then, barely two months old. His great claws were like a handful of sharp daggers. And his beak, oh! When you see a condor's beak as close up as I saw it, you never forget it!"

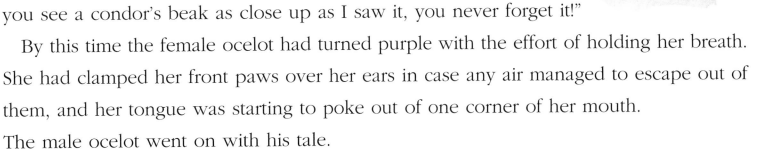

By this time the female ocelot had turned purple with the effort of holding her breath. She had clamped her front paws over her ears in case any air managed to escape out of them, and her tongue was starting to poke out of one corner of her mouth.
The male ocelot went on with his tale.

"I waited, terrified, for the condor to pounce, but he simply shuffled his feet. At last he asked me what I was doing beside the river, all by myself, so I told him what had happened. Condor stood there next to me, and he stared out at the great rushing river for ages and when he spoke his voice seemed as empty as the sky.

"'It was a terrible storm, it is true. It threw down our tree as if it were a piece of grass. Our nest was hurled into the river and my son, too young to fly, was swept away, much like you. You escaped, but he has gone.'

"Condor sighed and looked at me.

"'There has been too much grief today.'

63

"And then he picked me up in his claws, as gently as if I were his own child, and lifted me into the air. We flew and we flew until we came to the forest I recognised. There was my mother, howling beside the river bank, looking for her lost son. Condor drifted down and placed me beside her, and then he had gone. I was safe again and my mother and I wept with happiness and thanked Condor from the bottom of our hearts for his kindness. It was extraordinary."

The other animals nodded their heads. It was a miraculous story.

"Spluuuurrrrrgh!"

The female ocelot finally burst her lungs and her breath exploded from her body. She grinned at everyone.

"See?" she cried. "How's that?"

"Very good," they cheered. "Why don't you do it again?"

The Porcupine's Story

Michael Lawrence

"I would like to tell my story tonight," said a splendid porcupine, shuffling up to the front with his porcupine partner.

"I'm sure it will be very interesting," said Noah. "Please go ahead."

"I will," said the porcupine. "But before I begin, I should tell you that I've noticed how much you all admire my quills. They are magnificent, aren't they?"

"They're a bit too sharp for my liking," grunted a warthog.

"Well, you shouldn't get too close," said the porcupine, "or you might find yourself with an extra nostril or two. Quills as fine as mine are extremely sharp. Anyway, as I was about to tell you, there was a time when I didn't have half as many."

And this was the tale the porcupine told.

"Now I'm an active sort of fellow most of the year, but in winter I barely open my eyes till the last frosts have gone and the air warms up.

"There was one winter, however, when I was woken time and time again by a bad dream – the same dream each time – in which my quills were plucked from me by an unseen thief. A very painful dream it was too, but each time I woke and found everything as it should be I said, 'Oh, just a silly dream,' and tumbled back to sleep.

"It wasn't until the seventh or eighth rude awakening that I felt certain that something wasn't right. I didn't feel at all myself. I shuffled to a puddle and looked in. And oh my, what a sight met my eyes: almost half my wonderful quills had disappeared!"

"Oh no!" gasped the rabbits. "Who had taken them, Porcupine?"

"What a nasty thing to do," squealed the guinea pigs.

"Shush now," said an elephant. "Let Porcupine tell his story."

"I looked about me," continued Porcupine. "Perhaps they'd fallen out while I tossed and turned in my sleep. But not a single quill was there to be seen. Where could they have got to? Not outside, surely? I ran to the little hole in the wall that lets the daylight in. I peered out. No, no quills out there either – and it was snowing. Brrrr. I went back to bed.

"I can't say how much time passed before my next dream. You know how it is with dreams; weeks might pass between them or no time at all. But when it came it was the same old painful dream. I woke with the usual start and went to the puddle. I looked in. So few quills had I now that I looked more like a common sewer rat than a noble porcupine. Sorry, Rat, no offence," said Porcupine, turning to face a rather cross-looking rodent in the corner.

"I peered through the hole in the wall. The snow had gone. There were flowers and young grass, and new leaves on the trees. Spring had come. Time to go out and find food.

"Keeping under cover to avoid being seen in my half-naked state, I took my food where I found it, moving forward as I ate, hardly lifting my snout from the ground. Suddenly I heard voices. I stopped. I looked up. I had come to one of the villages of Man. I concealed myself at once. Humans can be dangerous. From my hiding place I saw a man selling things from a market stall, with people crowding round, eager to buy. He was selling pots and pans, curtain material, firewood, herbs, dried fruit and ... porcupine quill toothpicks."

"Ooh!" shrieked the guinea pigs.

"I was so amazed that, at first, I didn't notice the bird on the stall-keeper's shoulder. It was a magpie, and each time someone asked for some toothpicks it would flutter down, seize a bundle in its beak, and offer the quills to the customer, who would laugh with delight at the bird's cleverness.

"So all my bad dreams had not been dreams at all! The magpie had crept into my home while I slept and torn my quills from me for its master to sell as toothpicks!

"The magpie must have heard my snort of rage, for it glanced my way, and such was its panic when it saw me that it spun round on its master's shoulder and beaked his cheek. The man howled with pain and stumbled into his stall. It went flying. So did everything on it. Porcupine quill toothpicks rained down like arrows on his customers, who turned on him in fury, while the stall-keeper turned on the bird whose beak had caused the upset.

"The magpie might have been a sly bird, but it wasn't a stupid one. It flew beyond its master's furious reach, flew high and fast, and I never saw it again – till now. Yes, I see you magpies, hiding there in the elephant's ear. It might interest you to know that I too fled that angry village in haste. For many unhappy days I travelled, always under cover to hide my shame from curious eyes, wondering what was to become of me in my sorry condition.

"One morning it started to rain. Just a drizzle at first, but the drizzle quickly became the downpour that would become the Great Rain, which would bring the Great Flood, which would cover the world and bring us here to the Ark. I cast about me for shelter. I saw a forest. A pine forest. I raced towards it. By the time I reached it the ground was nothing but mud. Very soft, very slippery mud. I lost my footing. Over I went – *squelch!* – and slithered and bounced and rolled into the forest like a ball.

"When I came to a halt and got to my feet, I found that the forest floor had a carpet of pine needles, many of which had attached themselves to me. I laughed. I couldn't help it. Well, it had its funny side. Pine needles for a porcupine! A coat of pine needles would certainly do till my quills grew back – which as you see they've now done. And aren't they grand? Aren't they fine? Better even than the last lot, I'd say. I wouldn't want to lose these. So you'll understand why I'll be sleeping with one eye open from now on – especially with a thieving magpie on board."

The Bee and the Wasp's Story

Vivian French

"I can hear a bee and a wasp buzzing at each other," said Noah. "Why don't you tell us a story instead?"

"BUZZZ!!!" said Bee. "Wasps don't know anything about anything!"

Wasp glared at Bee and flicked his wings.

"Oh yes we do! We know how you bees tricked us wasps!"

"We did NOT!" Bee said. "YOU were the ones who wanted stings!"

"Now, now," said Noah. "What's all this about?"

"It happened a long time ago," said Wasp grumpily, "when bees AND wasps made honey."

"Wasp honey was always poor stuff," Bee interrupted.

"Shush, Bee," said Noah.

"AS I WAS SAYING," Wasp said loudly, "wasps used to make honey as well as bees. And VERY GOOD HONEY it was, too. But we both had trouble with the human beings.

They were always rootling and trampling and scrambling and scraping around our trees trying to get our honey ..."

"Don't forget those dreadful fires!" said Bee. "They were the worst of all."

Wasp nodded.

"They brought damp sticks and made horrible smoky fires so we couldn't breathe – we had to fly away –"

"– and while we were gone they stole ALL the honey!" said Bee. "It was TERRIBLE!"

"It was DREADFUL!" Wasp agreed. "We had to do something about it. We called a meeting."

"And THAT was when the wasps thought of the stings," Bee said. "You see, we didn't have stings when we were first made. ALL the animals and the human beings were meant to be friends together."

Noah sighed.

"I remember. No fighting. No killing. Everyone happy. No moaning. No telling lies."

"And no stealing other people's honey," Wasp said firmly. "But they did. So we flew back up to God's front door and we asked for stings. BIG stings that would make big red bumps on people's noses."

"But God said we had to choose," said Bee. "He said EITHER we could go on making honey, OR we could have stings."

Wasp buzzed crossly.

"That was when we were tricked. The bees said they'd make honey if we wasps did the stinging … and we could share the honey between us. But then they sneaked back to God with a bowl of sweet golden sticky honeycomb – and God liked it so much that he gave the bees stings too! So we wasps made a promise that we would never ever EVER speak to bees again. ZZZZZZ!!! And we never have – well, not until we were squashed together in this Ark!! But once we get out – ZZZZZZ!!!!"

Bee sighed.

"But didn't you know, Wasp? Our stings aren't any good to us. If we DO sting anyone then we die."

Wasp stopped buzzing and stared at Bee.

"Is that true?"

Bee nodded.

"Is that REALLY true?" Wasp asked Noah.

Noah nodded.

"OHO!!!!" said Wasp, and he began to shake with laughter.

"Wasp!" said Noah, shocked. "That's not kind!"

"No," said Wasp. "It's not … but it's a good joke, isn't it? *There's a sting in the tail in the tale of the sting!!!!*"

And Wasp flew off in a series of cheerful loops.

The Wolf's Story

Michael Lawrence

"There's a wolf growling away over there," said Noah. "I wish you'd stop it – it's upsetting all sorts of animals. Why don't you entertain us with a story instead?"

"I know what you're after," snarled the wolf. "You want me to tell you about that business with the three little pigs, don't you? Well, I will. I'll tell you what really happened, and you'll see that I'm not the bad chap I've been made out to be."

The pigs backed away into a corner, looking rather anxious, and the wolf began his story.

"I was on holiday down south when I heard about three little pigs who lived in houses. How quaint, thought I, and headed down the road to see this curiosity for myself. Before long I came to a house of straw, and in the garden there was a little pig sunbathing. A very untidy garden it was, quite overgrown, all nettles, not a flower in sight.

"'Good day little pig!' I called. 'Wolf's the name! Allow me to shake your trotter with a friendly furry paw!'

"But on hearing my cheery greeting the little pig sprang up and cried, 'It's the Big Bad Wolf, the Big Bad Wolf, come to trick me and gobble me up!'

"'Trick you?'" I said. 'Gobble you up? You mistake me for one of your southern wolves. We northern wolves aren't in the gobbling game. We wouldn't hurt a fly. Or even a pig.'

"'You can't fool me,' he replied, skipping into his house. 'You're all the same, you wolves. Keep your distance or I'll call my big brothers. They only live along the road.'

"Well, naturally I would have defended myself further, but just then my nose began to twitch and I felt a sneeze coming on. I should tell you that I never sneeze, never ever, even when the pepper trees are in bloom. But here one came, and a mighty powerful sneeze at that.

"So great and calamitous a sneeze it was that it flung me over on my back, flat out. And what do you think I found when I raised my poor sneezed-out head from the ground? Why, the little house in ruins and the poor pig sitting all dazed and doolally in the straw.

"Well, I rushed to help the dear wee beast, but when he saw me coming he squealed and jumped up, so dizzy and tottery that he dived the wrong way – into the very jaws that were coming to his aid. Past my teeth he scooted, down my throat, and into my rumbly old tum before I knew what was what.

"And that, my friends, was the end of him. Very sad, but not my fault, you'll agree?"

The two little rabbits at Noah's feet glanced at each other nervously.

"When the little piggy-wig stopped moving about in my tummy-tum-tum," continued Wolf, "I said to myself, 'I must go and tell his brothers what occurred here and shed a tear with them.'

"So along the road I slunk till I came to the house of the second little pig. This house was made not of straw but of twigs, though again the garden was nothing but nettles. The second little pig was up a ladder cleaning his windows.

"'Good day, little pig!' I said, drawing near. 'Wolf's the name! Come down and let me shake your trotter with a friendly, furry paw and tell you my unfortunate news.'

"But the little pig cried, 'It's the Big Bad Wolf, the Big Bad Wolf, come to trick me and gobble me up!' And he jumped off his ladder, into his house by way of the window.

"'What suspicious little pigs you are round here,' said I. 'As I told your brother before the accident, I'm not that kind of wolf at all.'

"'Accident?' said the ruffled pig from his window.

"I explained, then asked if I could come in and weep with him.

"'Not a chance,' said he. 'I see your plan. Once in my house you'll wolf me down too, like my poor little brother.'

"'No, no, no, no,' I replied. 'I'm a northern wolf, the salt of the earth, I'm not like your –'

"But before I could finish, my nose began to twitch and I felt another mighty sneeze coming on, and next thing I knew …

AAAH… TI…. SHOO!

I fell over on my back, and when next I looked there was the little pig, all dazed and doolally among the sticks of his ruined house.

"Well, I ran at once to calm him, but when he saw me coming he squealed and jumped up, all dizzy and tottery, and like his poor brother lurched the wrong way, past my teeth, down my throat, and into my rumbly old tummy-tum-tum.

"What a tragic day this was turning out to be!

"When the second little piggy-wig stopped moving about, I licked my sad old lips and said, 'I must go and tell the last little pig what occurred here and shed a tear or two with him.'

"The third little pig's house wasn't made of straw and it wasn't made of sticks; it was made of brick, but his garden was just as bad as the others, nettles from front to back and end to end. He was oiling the hinges on the gate as I strolled up.

"'Good day, little pig! Wolf's the name! Allow me to shake your trotter with a friendly furry –'

"That was as far as I got before the third little pig threw his oilcan in the air and skedaddled up the path.

"'It's the Big Bad Wolf, the Big Bad Wolf, come to trick me and gobble me up!'

"'Wait!' I cried. 'I have news of your brothers down the road!'

"He paused at this and I told him from the gate what had happened through no fault of my own. But alas and alack, he slammed the door and bolted it against me. I sighed, but still wishing to make my peace with him I sauntered up the path. I was about to knock on the door when my nose began to twitch, and …

"But this time when I raised my befuddled sneezed-out head from the ground it wasn't to find the little pig all dazed and doolally in the ruins of his house. No, this time the house was still standing and the little pig still inside it, bless his little cotton socks.

"'You won't blow *my* house down,' he said. 'Not if you huff and puff till the milk goes off or sneeze and wheeze till the sky falls in. Away with you, Big Bad Wolf, be gone! And if it crosses your mind to come down my chimney because it's the only way to get in, you'll regret it and don't say I didn't warn you.'

"'Now that's an idea,' thought I. 'I'll talk to him down the chimney. I'm sure he'll realise I mean no harm if I persist.'

"So I climbed up the drainpipe and hollered down the chimney.

"'Little pig, little pig, let me come in, I'm your pal, I swear by your chinny-chin-chin.'

"But answer came there none, so I climbed into the chimney and slipped down through the sooty dark, as keen as mustard to prove what a charming chap I am.

"Oh, but what do you think I found when I tumbled into the hearth? A colossal cauldron of water just coming to the boil, that's what. And into it I plopped, to be scalded through and through and inside out. But that wasn't the worst of it, dear me no. When I leapt from the pot with an agonised roar the sly little pig began to beat my brain to bacon with an iron frying pan.

"I ran to the door.

"I ran up the path.

"I ran through the freshly-oiled gate and up the road, and northward, never to venture into the inhospitable south again.

"There, now you see how misjudged I've been, what a good-hearted fellow I …

"Excuse me, is that a pig I see among you? Indeed it is, and a very special pig too if I'm not mistaken. Delighted to meet you again, little pig. No hard feelings, you see. But what's that you have there? A bouquet of nettles? How unusual. Sorry, what was that? The old hearing isn't what it was since someone beat me almost senseless with a frying pan for trying to be nice to him. You always carry nettles because they keep Big Bad Wolves away? Ho-ho, what a jolly little porker you are. Come closer, let me see them properly, let me have a … sniff.

"Oh dear. A tickle seems to have entered my honest nose. I think I'm going to … ah … ah … ah …

"I really must apologise, everyone. Can't think what brought that on. Here, let me help you all up. You first, *dear* little pig."

Day 13

The Moth's Story

Adèle Geras

"After all that commotion last night I think we need a calming story," said Noah the next evening. "Moth, tell us your story. Don't be shy!"

The moth fluttered up to his shoulder. "Can you hear me?" she asked. "I know I've only got a tiny voice, and that my words may drift away before you catch them. But if you listen carefully, you'll find that I have had some terrifying adventures that would make other moths tremble."

"Please tell us," said Noah. "We're all ears." And Moth began.

"I spent my early days safely tucked in the folds of a blanket made of wool. My moth brothers were there for company, and we had a happy time, all of us, chewing and nibbling in the warm darkness.

"Then, one day, the thing happened that every moth fears and dreads: a blanketshake. Do you know what that is? The wool you are sitting on is taken by human hands and flung about so that it buckles and moves, and you are tossed … that's the only word for it …

up into the air, along with all your companions and the dustmites and fleas who shared the blanket with you, not knowing where you are, or what is happening or why your safe woolly home has suddenly disappeared.

"My wings were new and untried, but I learned to fly in a hurry. I had to. We all did.

I flew as far as my wings would flutter, and then I landed. I was lucky.

"I found myself on a wide, striped rug, and, joy of joys, it was made of wool. I was just having a nibble to give myself some strength, when a human being began to roll up the rug.

"First a blanketshake and then a rugroll … it was too much for one day. I folded my wings and decided to wait.

"I must have dozed off, and while I slept I dreamed of rain, falling and falling and pattering on the earth. I only woke up when the rug was unrolled again. And here I am, sitting on it, and here are all of you, sitting nearby and telling one another stories.

"I'm glad I had the chance to speak of my adventures, because now I have to go. Do you see that lamp hanging over there? I must move closer to it. The golden flame is calling me, and I must fly to be near it. Thank you, my friends, for listening to me. I am gone. I am gone to the warmth that lives in the heart of the light. Goodbye."

83

The Elephant's Story

Jean Ure

"Tonight's a big night," said Noah. "The elephants are going to let us in on a secret."

"As you know," said the big grey elephant, "we elephants have remarkable memories … an elephant never forgets! But it wasn't always so. Once upon a time, elephants had perfectly ordinary memories, the same as anyone else. Now, of course, we have the longest and the best memories of any animal. I will tell you how it came about."

The elephant paused.

"Are you sitting comfortably?"

All the animals nodded.

"Then I shall begin. One day, in the forest, a little elephant was born."

"What was his name?" asked a guinea pig.

"I don't know his name. I shall call him Little Elephant. Now, poor Little Elephant had no memory at all! His mother despaired of him.

"'Little Elephant,' she would say, 'make sure you're back by tea time.'

"And Little Elephant would run off to play and quite forget what his mother had said. He would turn up at bedtime and wonder why she was cross with him.

"Other times she would send him into the forest to collect leaves for supper, and Little Elephant would come back with a mouthful of flowers, instead.

"'I thought you would like them, mama!'

"And his mother did like them, but they were not what she had asked for! And then of course, there wasn't anything for supper, and Little Elephant's father would bang his trunk on the ground and shout, 'This is not good enough! What is the matter with the child?'

"Nobody knew. But poor Little Elephant couldn't remember the simplest thing!

"One day he was trundling through the forest, humming a little song to himself, when he met a snake slithering through the grass.

"'Hey, Little Elephant!' cried the snake. 'I jussst bumped into a ssspider monkey… there'ssss a fire coming thisss way. You'd bessst get back and warn your folksss!'

"'A fire!' thought Little Elephant. "He'd heard about fires. They roared through the forest, consuming everything in their path. Help, help! He must get back and warn his folks!

"But how was he to remember? Little Elephant's memory was so bad that by the time he got back he was bound to have forgotten!

"'I know,' thought Little Elephant. 'I'll tie a knot in my trunk. That will remind me!'

"So he tied a knot in his trunk, and felt very pleased and proud.

"'Now I shall remember!' thought Little Elephant, as he galloped on his way.

"But, oh dear! Before he was even half way home, he had already forgotten what he was galloping for!

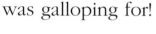

"He saw a clump of berries which looked good to eat, and so he stopped a while to eat them. While he was eating, a butterfly fluttered past.

"'Hey, Little Elephant!' cried the butterfly. 'I've just met a beetle … there's a fire coming this way. You'd best get back and warn your folks!'

"'A fire!' thought Little Elephant. "He'd heard about fires. They roared through the forest, consuming everything in their path. Help, help! He must get back and warn his folks!

"But how was he to remember?

"'I know!' thought Little Elephant. 'I'll tie a knot in my trunk. That will remind me!'

"So he tied a second knot in his trunk and went galloping on his way. As he galloped he thought, 'Fire, fire! Help, fire!' Surely if he kept saying it to himself, he would remember?

"But, oh dear! Before he was even half way home, he caught his foot in a root and came crashing down – and clean forgot what he was galloping for!

"'Ouch,' thought Little Elephant. 'That hurt!'

"As he stood there, rubbing his foot, a parrot flew screeching past.

"'Hey, Little Elephant!' cried the parrot. 'I just heard from a chimpanzee … there's a fire coming this way. You'd best get back and warn your folks!'

"'A fire!' thought Little Elephant. He'd heard about fires. They roared through the forest, consuming everything in their path. He must get back and warn his folks!

"But how was he to remember?

"'I know,' thought Little Elephant. 'I'll tie a knot in my trunk. That will remind me!'

"So he tied a third knot in his trunk and went galloping on his way.

"'You'd better hurry!' squawked the parrot. 'It's nearly on top of us!'

"Little Elephant was really frightened. He blundered on, through the forest, while the parrot flew overhead screeching at him.

"'Fire, fire!' screeched the parrot. 'Get a move on!'

"At last Little Elephant reached the clearing where his mum and dad, his brothers and sisters, and his grandma and grandpa, and the aunties and uncles were all nibbling greenery.

"'Fire, fire!' shouted Little Elephant.

"'Fire, fire!' screeched the parrot.

"All the elephants raised their heads and sniffed at the air. Then the mums and dads, and the grandmas and grandpas, and the his aunties and uncles all waved their trunks and trumpeted FIRE! And the whole herd turned and went galloping off through the forest. And as they galloped, the fire galloped along behind them, consuming everything in its path."

Here the elephant broke off to give a cuddle to the two little guinea pigs, who were looking rather scared.

"It's all right, darlings! The fire didn't catch them. They were safe! Little Elephant had warned them just in time.

"When the panic was over, and the fire had died away, Little Elephant's mother turned to him and said, 'Little Elephant! What a mess your trunk is in. Why have you tied so many knots in it?'

"'I can't remember,' said Little Elephant.

"'Let me untie them for you,' said his mother.

"She untied the first knot; she untied the second knot; she untied the third knot – and suddenly Little Elephant remembered!

"'It was to remind me to tell you about the fire!'

"All the elephants were tremendously impressed. For the first time in his life, Little Elephant had remembered something! And from that day on, all the elephants started tying knots in their trunks, and that is the reason elephants have such amazing memories. And also," added the elephant, "the reason we have so many wrinkles in our trunks. It's from tying all those knots!"

One of the guinea pigs was tugging at the elephant's ear.

"Yes, darling?" said the elephant.

"Is it the reason human beings tie knots in their handkerchiefs?"

"Very likely it is," said the elephant. "They are trying to give themselves good memories. But nothing works as well as a trunk!"

The Cat's Story

Michael Lawrence

The two cats were sitting next to Noah, preening themselves as usual.

"Why don't you stop that for a moment and tell us a cat story?" said Noah.

The black cat stopped licking her paws and looked up.

"Very well," she announced. "Is everybody listening? Then I'll tell you what it's like to be a cat. Humans seem to think that black cats are lucky. I don't know where they get that idea. I've never been so lucky."

And the cat began her story.

"The day I came onto the Ark, a nearby elephant noticed a nearby mouse. Elephants do not like mice. He stepped back in haste – onto my tail. I squealed. I tried to pull my tail out. It didn't budge. I pulled harder. Suddenly the elephant lifted his clumping great foot. I shot into a sack of flour, which made me sneeze.

"So heartily did I sneeze that I flew head over poor squashed tail onto the point of a warthog's tusk. I did not linger there, but leapt smartly into a coil of rope which one of Noah's sons was just about to tug. The rope flicked me up into the sky, very high, all the way to the crow's nest, where the crow unkindly pecked my bottom.

"Now down I tumbled, down and down, and where did I land? Why, in a convenient pan of pigswill! I crawled out of the foul muck that pigs call lunch just in time to be flattened by an opening door, from where I fell into the path of a stampeding buffalo.

"Reeling (just a little) I sought a safe place to claw the splinters from my nose. Ah – a water barrel! I had just reached the rim of the barrel when a passing camel burped, which caused a goat to jump, which caused a snake to hiss, which caused a lion to roar, which caused a donkey to kick me into the barrel, where I might have drowned if Noah hadn't fished me out.

"Noah is rather fond of me. It was he who gave me my name when he first saw me. What name? Oh, didn't I say? It's Lucky. Noah calls me Lucky."

The two little rabbits started giggling. Cat threw them a withering glare and went back to licking her paws.

The Hamster's Story

Jeremy Strong

"Whose turn is it tonight?" said Noah.

The hamster began to give little hops. She squeaked quietly, almost as if she were talking to herself. Her tiny ears twitched and flicked as though they were being tickled. Suddenly she ran straight into the circle that had been formed by the animals. She blurted out, "I had a dream last night!" then dashed away and hid beneath the warm feathers of a hen.

The other animals were stunned. They stared at the hen, who began to shuffle uncomfortably.

"I never said a word," she clucked. "It was the hamster. Come out, Hamster, and tell us your dream."

A small nose appeared beneath the brown feathers, and two black-as-night eyes.

96

The hamster crept slowly back to the centre of the circle. The female ocelot watched the hamster with half-closed eyes. The big cat sighed.

"Hamsters cannot dream," she announced.

"I had a dream!" the hamster repeated.

"Your brain is far too small to have dreams," said the female ocelot. "Only intelligent creatures, such as myself, can dream."

"I had a dream!" insisted the hamster, who was beginning to get cross.

The female ocelot flicked out her claws and flashed them in front of the hamster.

"You are an argumentative rodent. I could kill you with a single swipe of my paw, and eat you with one crunch of my jaws."

The hamster bravely stood her ground.

"It is a fact that you could easily kill me, Ocelot, but even if you do kill me it won't change another fact, and that is that I HAD A DREAM LAST NIGHT!"

The hamster leaped in the air as she shouted at the ocelot, and the big cat stepped back several paces. The other creatures laughed to see the ocelot so taken aback. The female ocelot was gracious enough to admit defeat.

"All right, little hamster," she purred, "tell us your dream."

And the hamster began.

"I was being chased amongst the leaves and roots of the forest floor. Some terrifying creature was after me. Just as it leaped upon me I jumped too, into the air. I felt myself flying. And then I was in a strange place. The floor was like the forest but it smelled fresh and new. I ran forward and came to a wall. I ran to the side and I came to a wall. I looked up and there was a roof, high above my head.

"The strangest thing was that I felt utterly safe. In one corner was a big pile of wood shavings. It was so warm and snug, the most wonderful nest you could imagine. And in another corner was such a strange thing – a kind of round thing that turned.

I climbed inside and I tried to run up it, but it turned and the faster I ran the faster it turned, faster and faster. It was so funny! I was laughing so much I fell out, and that was what woke me up. I had fallen out of my sleeping place, and I was still laughing."

The hamster's eyes were shining as she looked up at the other animals.

"It was the happiest dream I have ever had," she sighed.

The Lioness's Story

Jenny Nimmo

"We're very lucky tonight. The lioness has agreed to tell us her story," said Noah.

There was a shuffling and a shushing among the animals, and some of them backed away as the two lions padded into the middle of the story circle. The lion lay down for a doze and the lioness began her story.

"This is a story about a little lion called Mali.

"When Mali was a cub her mother disappeared. The family had been without food for a week and the big lioness knew that if her children weren't fed very soon, they would die.

"She decided to hunt at night. Her two cubs would be safer if she left them in the dark. They wouldn't be seen by the fierce animals that roamed the savannah where they lived.

"'Don't make a sound until I come back,' said the lioness. 'If I'm not here at sunrise you must go and find the rest of our family. You'll be safe with them.'

"The cubs watched their mother walk through the gap in the rocks where they were hiding.

When she had gone they could see the moon, huge and golden, hanging in the dark sky.

"'I'm going to help our mother,' said Ramo, Mali's brother.

"Mali gave a little growl.

"'It isn't safe for cubs out there.'

"'I'm bigger than you,' said Ramo. 'I'm going to hunt for myself.' And he bounded into the darkness.

"Mali listened to the strange noises of the night. The howls and hoots, the squeaks and growls. Lonely and frightened, she huddled against the rocks and fell asleep.

"When Mali woke, she was still alone. It was dawn and her mother and brother hadn't returned. She knew then that she would never see them again. If she wanted to survive she would have to find another family.

"Mali crept through the rocks until she could see the savannah, a great dusty plain dotted with scrubby trees and bushes. She had been out there before, but never alone. I must be brave, she thought, and leapt from the rocks.

"For two days and two nights Mali walked through the savannah. When the sun was high and the ground trembled with heat, she slept, hidden in the undergrowth. On the second night she found a dead bird. It was very small but it was a meal. It gave Mali a little strength. And hope. She kept moving and as dawn broke she caught a familiar scent on the air, the scent of a lion.

"With all the strength left in her body, Mali bounded towards that scent. She was met by an angry snarl. Three lion cubs were playing together in a sandpit: a male and two females. As Mali looked down on them, one of the females growled, 'Go away!'

"'I'm hungry,' said Mali.

"'We're hungry too,' said the other female.

"'But you have food,' said Mali, 'I can smell it.'

"There was, indeed, a large piece of meat on the bank behind the cubs. Mali began to crawl down the bank towards the meat.

"With a roar the two females rushed at Mali. She leapt away and sank on to the grass above the sandpit. She lay there all day, too exhausted to move, her head on her paws, her eyes closed. At length she slept.

"When Mali woke up she found the cubs licking her face.

"'Sorry! Sorry!' they murmured. 'We didn't mean to be cruel. We want you to live. Come, eat!'

"Mali crawled over to the meat and together they ate. She felt so much better. She wasn't alone any more, and the food had given her strength. She was happy. And then one of the female cubs said, 'You must leave here now. Our father is returning. We can smell him. He won't permit strangers.'

"'But I'm not …' Mali began.

"'He will not permit it!' the cub repeated. 'Now you have eaten you are strong. You must go. You must find a new place.'

"Mali looked at the cubs in despair. How could she go on, alone?

"The male cub spoke.

"'I am leaving, too,' he said. 'Our father is cruel. He doesn't like me because I am male. He might even kill me. My name is Zimi.'

"All at once the world didn't seem so frightening to Mali. The cubs said farewell to each other, and then Mali and Zimi began their journey into the vast, unknown world. They walked a little apart but, somehow, they were together."

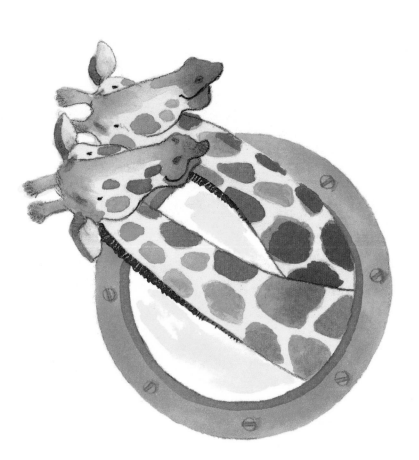

Day 18

The Giraffe's Story

Adèle Geras

A giraffe bent down her long neck and whispered in Noah's ear.

"A poem? Of course you can give us a poem," said Noah. "Come here, everyone. Our tall friend says giraffes don't know any stories, so she'll recite a poem instead."

So the giraffe began.

"I
am the
tallest
animal in
the whole of
the world.
I look down at the tops
of all the trees
and the leaves are
like a dark green sea,
foaming around me.
It's hard for a giraffe
to be shut in this Ark.
I have to fold my legs
and sit and sit.
I like to stand on the deck
and look at the moon
and the silver stripe it lays
on the water.
A long, stripe, like my long neck."

The Sparrow's Story

Alan Durant

"Excuse me, Noah," boomed an eagle. "Do you realize you haven't asked a single bird to tell a story? It's disgraceful!"

"That's right!" twittered a magpie. "There are lots of us here. We ought to be allowed!"

"Fine!" said Noah. "Who will begin?"

"I will," chirped a sparrow, and he fluttered down and settled on the ear of a hippo, ready to begin his story.

"High on the branch of a tall tree, at the edge of a dark forest, lived a little sparrow. He had no family, he had no friends and he was lonely. All day he sat on his branch watching the other birds fly in the air and among the leafy trees of the forest. Everyone, it seemed, had a friend, but him.

"Summer turned to autumn. The leaves turned from green to brown and fell to the ground. High on his branch, the little sparrow grew sadder.

He watched the swallows gather in the sky, then soar away gracefully together to sunnier lands. The little sparrow sighed.

"'Ah, if only I could fly so gracefully,' he said to himself. 'Then I would have a friend for sure.'

"He flapped his wings and hopped into the air, but he could not soar gracefully like the swallows.

"Winter came. Snow fell. The little sparrow shivered on his branch. Down below a robin sat on a log, his breast as red and beautiful as a ruby. Soon, another robin flew down and sat on the log beside him. They chirped merrily together. The little sparrow watched.

"'Ah, if only I had a beautiful red breast,' he said to himself. 'Then I would have a friend for sure.'

"He opened his beak and sang. But the notes that came were thin and shrill. The little sparrow hung his head and, sadly, went to sleep.

"Next morning, when the little sparrow awoke, he looked down and saw something long and fat, wriggling in the snow: a worm. The little sparrow was very hungry. With a hop and a flap, he flew down to the ground.

"It was the longest, wriggliest, most enormous worm the little bird had ever seen. Further and further it stretched across the snow. Further and further and further … and there, at the end, was another little bird that looked just like him!

"The little sparrow blinked. His beak opened and the worm fell out.

"'Oh,' he cried.

"'Oh,' cried the other little bird.

"They stared at one another.

"'Please,' cheeped the little sparrow, 'after you.'

"'Oh no,' cheeped the other little bird, 'after you.'

"But when they looked down, the worm had gone!

"'I have some grubs in my nest, if you'd care to share them,' peeped the other little bird shyly.

"'Oh, yes, please,' chirped the little sparrow.

"So, twittering and tweeting, the two little birds flew away together into the forest.

"At last the little sparrow was happy. He could not soar like a swallow. He did not have a beautiful red breast like a robin. He could not sing as sweetly as the nightingale. But he had all that he wanted.

"He had a friend."

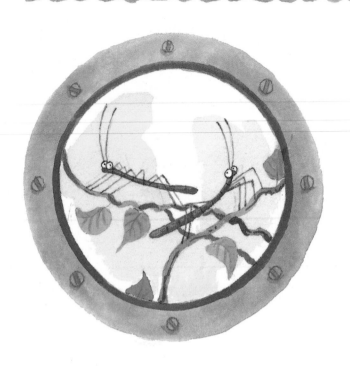

The Stick Insect's Story

Jeremy Strong

"A funny thing happened to me once," said a stick insect. "Can I tell you about it, Noah, please?"

"Of course you can," said Noah, even though the stick insect sounded like a duck with a sore throat. In fact, a duck who had a bit of a sore throat at the time, thought that Stick Insect was making fun of her. Duck huffily turned her back.

"I was sitting on a branch, minding my own business, when BAM! Out of the sky swooped a jackdaw. He grabbed me in his beak and flew off. There I was, jammed in his beak and thinking I was as good as dead. But I told myself to keep very still and behave as if nothing had happened, so I carried on pretending to be a stick.

"Anyhow, we seemed to fly for miles and miles. Eventually the jackdaw dropped down to his nest, and there his mate was waiting for him. I was thinking, oh no, now I'm going to be eaten twice! But I still carried on pretending to be a stick.

"Well, the jackdaw handed me over to his mate and do you know what she did with me? Stuffed me into her nest. She did! She rammed me head first amongst all the other twigs. She thought I was really a stick!

"I was stuck there for weeks. I waited while she laid her eggs. I waited while the eggs hatched. I waited while the youngsters grew up. And all that time I was a stuck stick.

I didn't manage to escape until all the jackdaws left the nest. Then I wriggled out and made my getaway."

The stick insect gazed round at the listening faces. The jackdaw didn't seem very impressed.

"You made that up," he said and the stick insect grinned.

"That's what most stories are," he pointed out. "They're made up."

The Chameleon's Story

Jeremy Strong

"I know a sticky story too," announced a chameleon, rolling his eyes in two different directions at once.

The other animals began to giggle.

"It wasn't the least bit funny," he added.

"I'm sorry," murmured a giraffe. "It's just that, well, you look funny. You always look funny when you roll your eyes like that."

But the stick insect waved his feelers cheerily at the chameleon.

"Tell us your sticky story," he said.

The chameleon's eyes flicked from one animal to another, and when he was sure he had their undivided attention he began to unfold his sorry tale.

"I was out hunting, looking for something tasty. I kept very still, so that my prey wouldn't spot me and make an escape.

I can keep still for hours. Once I didn't move for three days."

"You must have been asleep," snarled a hyena.

"Of course I wasn't asleep," retorted the chameleon. "I was hunting, and I'll tell you something else. I have brilliant eyesight. If a juicy fly landed on Noah's head I could spot it from here. And not only could I see that fly, but I would be able to see each leg on the fly, and each knee on each leg."

The chameleon gazed round at everyone with a rather smug expression on his grizzled face.

"So what happened then?" asked a monkey, scratching at a little flea.

"I was standing near a bush," the chameleon continued. "It was a green and brown bush. I know it was green and brown because I changed colour. I can do that, you know. I can change colour. It's called …"

"Get on with the story!" squawked a parrot.

"I am an expert colour changer," droned the chameleon, closing one eye and keeping the other fixed on his audience. "I remember once I was half way up a tree. The bark of this tree was a browny-grey, so I made myself a browny-grey. But the leaves were bright green. So do you know what I did? I made my toes go green. My toes looked like leaves. Extraordinary. I'm clever like that, you know. I think about these little touches. It makes all the difference."

"Tell us your sticky story!" the lioness suddenly roared. "If you don't tell us your sticky story you'll come to a sticky end."

The chameleon seemed very surprised that the lioness should make such a fuss.

"How very impatient you are," he drawled. "I *am* telling you the story, and in order to tell the story properly I have to put in extra bits."

The lioness scowled and bared her fangs.

"I shall put some of my extra bits in you if you don't get a move on."

The other animals began sniggering again, but the chameleon was too involved in his own performance to notice.

"I was lying in wait, hoping for a nice juicy fly, or grasshopper, or stick insect to land me. Stick insects are very tasty, you know."

"Really?" grunted the stick insect, and he shifted himself a bit further from the chameleon.

"Yes, and I'll tell you something else. I catch them with my tongue. Have you seen my tongue? It is very long and sticky. I have to fold it up to get it into my mouth. It's quite tricky."

"It doesn't seem to stop you talking," the male ocelot said with a yawn.

"No. That's because I am clever. Now, you take a look at my tongue."

At this point the chameleon opened wide his scaly mouth and slowly unfolded his tongue. It came tumbling out of his mouth like a string of flags from a magician's sleeve. There was more and more and more of it. At last his tongue was at full stretch. It lay across the floor of the Ark, between the animals. They all stared at it, in considerable wonder.

"That is a long tongue," agreed the giraffe, whose own tongue was pretty enormous.

The chameleon folded his tongue back into his mouth.

"It is sticky too," he pointed out. "That is how I catch insects. I lie in wait. A fly comes near. Bzzzz! Bzzzz! The fly lands. Slowly I open my mouth. Wider, wider, wider still and then …"

The chameleon's tongue suddenly sprang from his mouth and then went straight back in again.

"My tongue comes shooting out. The fly sticks to my tongue. I pull it back into my mouth and that is my dinner."

The lioness drummed her claws on the wooden floor.

"I seem to remember, Chameleon, that when you started this story half an hour ago, or was it last week, or last year? When you started this story you were going to tell us something sticky."

"I am just getting to that part. I was waiting for a fly to land. Along it came. Bzzzz. It landed on a large log. I opened my mouth. My tongue came shooting out and SPLAT! The fly flew off at the very last moment. My tongue hit the log and stuck there."

"Your tongue stuck to the log?" repeated the monkey.

"Exactly."

The lioness began to smile.

"So you never caught the fly? You caught a log instead?"

The chameleon nodded silently. All the animals now had a picture in their minds of the chameleon with his huge tongue stuck firmly to a log. Most of them were giggling, but the chameleon carried on with his sorry tale.

"Several animals came by, but because my tongue was stuck to the log I couldn't speak. And because I couldn't speak I couldn't ask for help. And because I couldn't ask for help I stayed stuck.

"Eventually some people came along, looking for firewood. They picked up the log and didn't notice me dangling underneath, hanging by my tongue."

The chameleon stopped and glanced at all the animals in turn, fixing them with his rolling eyes.

"What happened?" asked an ostrich.

The chameleon sighed dramatically.

"I was thrown on the fire."

"You were thrown on the fire!"

A deathly hush fell upon the animals. This was terrible. To be thrown on the fire was a dreadful fate. They stared in horror at the chameleon, and his pop-eyes blinked back at them.

"Then what happened?" the lioness asked, hardly daring to enquire. Small tears were beginning to appear at the corners of some of the animals' eyes as they contemplated the chameleon's appalling fate. He gazed back at them all.

"I died," he croaked.

"You died? Oh no!" wailed the animals. The female ocelot buried her face in her paws, but a little hamster was rolling across the floor in hysterics.

"How can the chameleon have died? He's just been telling us stories!"

The others sat up and looked at each other. That chameleon! What a joker!

"You tricked us," roared the lioness, but the chameleon was already lying on his back, kicking his thick legs in the air, and shaking with laughter.

Day 22

The Bear's Story

Lucy Coats

The next night a large brown bear rose to his feet.

"I would like to tell my story," he said.

"As long as it's not another sticky one!" laughed Noah, and the monkeys giggled.

"It isn't," the bear said. "It's rather sad."

"Not so long ago and not so far away, the Bear Woman sat in her cave on a mountain top and watched the worlds go by. The moon rose and fell and rose again and still the Bear Woman sat, dreaming and weaving, weaving and dreaming. And into her mind came a memory of green lands and great forests and of a white she-bear and a great warrior."

"Who is the Bear Woman?" demanded a hamster.

But Bear had a faraway look in his eyes by now and hadn't heard the hamster.

"It was a time when Man was destroying the Earth. He burned the trees and poisoned the land, and all the animals and birds and insects became frightened and went into hiding in the deepest forests where Man never went, and where the white she-bear called She-Who-Dances-The-Moonlight was queen.

"'She-Who-Dances-The-Moonlight will protect us,' said the creatures, and so she did. But Man's crops failed in the poisoned land, and he became hungry. There were no creatures to feed him, or keep him warm, and soon he began to starve. Then Man summoned a great warrior, whose name was Fat Foot.

"'Go into the forest and find me food!' commanded Man.

"So Fat Foot took his pack, his bow and arrows and set off into the forests to find food for Man.

"It was very dark, and Fat Foot became hopelessly lost. The birds fluttered round his head so that he couldn't see; the animals got under his feet and tripped him up; the insects got under his clothes and stung him till he danced about and howled with pain.

"Eventually he came into a clearing with a shining pool set right in the middle of it. The moon was full, and Fat Foot plunged thankfully into the cooling water, scattering moonbeams as he went. Suddenly he heard a terrible growl, and looking up he saw an enormous white she-bear standing at the edge of the water.

"'How dare you enter my Moon Pool!' she rumbled.

"Fat Foot was so frightened that he stumbled up out of the water and ran for his life. But She-Who-Dances-The-Moonlight was too quick for him. Her great furry, white paws danced across the moonbeams on the surface of the pool, and she leapt out onto Flat Foot's back.

"'OOOF!' said Fat Foot as he thumped down on the hard ground, expecting to be eaten up at any moment. The bear's great weight settled down on him, and suddenly she began to laugh.

"'Is this the greatest warrior Man can send against me?' she asked. 'This skinny little bag of bones? Get up, and tell me what your Master wants.'

"Fat Foot crawled out from under the queen's paws, and knelt before her.

"'Man is starving!' he stammered. 'He needs food, and he sent me to find it. But I have been blinded and tripped and bitten by your creatures, and I don't think there *is* any food in this horrible great dark forest!'

"She-Who-Dances-The-Moonlight looked at Fat Foot and shook her head.

"'Why should I help Man?' she asked. 'He has burned the trees and poisoned the land. If he is starving it's his own fault!'

"Fat Foot looked at her.

"'If you will help me, I promise to make Man behave,' he said. 'And if I don't then you can eat me!'

The bear queen laughed again as she lifted Fat Foot's chin with her great white paw, and stared deep into his eyes.

"'A bag of bones like you wouldn't make half a meal!' she chuckled. 'But I will help you anyway.'

"So She-Who-Dances-The-Moonlight summoned all the birds and animals and insects, and asked them to show Fat Foot how to find food in the forest. The birds showed him how to find seeds, grains and berries; the animals showed him how to find nuts and dig up roots; the insects showed him sweet honey and nectar.

And when his pack was full, Fat Foot took all the food back to Man and gave it to him.

"'Scrunch! Crunch! Munch!' went Man as he gobbled all the food up, leaving none for Fat Foot. 'What took you so long?'

"As Fat Foot explained his bargain with the bear queen, Man became very angry.

"Fat Foot tried and tried for a whole month to make Man behave, but the harder he tried the louder Man shouted and stamped his feet.

"'This is *my* land, and these are *my* trees and I shall do exactly what I like!' he roared, and his voice echoed round the land until even She-Who-Dances-The-Moonlight could hear him deep in her forest lair.

"Then Fat Foot was very sad, because he knew that Man would never listen to him, and now he would have to go back into the forest and be eaten up by She-Who-Dances-The-Moonlight. So he picked up his empty pack and his bow and arrows and set off to find her. This time he knew the way.

The birds came and sat on his shoulders and sang to him; the animals rubbed their furry heads against him; the insects fanned his hot head with their whirring wings.

"At last he came to the Moon Pool. It was a full moon once more, and as he watched, She-Who-Dances-The-Moonlight came towards him, sliding her great white paws across the moon's reflection in the water without disturbing it by so much as a hair.

"'Man will not behave,' said Fat Foot. 'So I have come to fulfil my part of the bargain.'

"The great bear queen smiled, showing her huge glittering white teeth. Then she began to dance. She danced in the silver moonlight, she danced in the shadows, she danced and danced until Fat Foot could stay still no longer, and he began to dance with her. On and on and on they danced, until Fat Foot began to change. His pack and bow and arrows dropped away and melted into the ground, and his nose began to grow longer. His hands changed into great silver tipped paws, and his ears became round and covered in hair. He opened his mouth and roared at the moon, and the bear queen took his paw and drew him towards the Moon Pool. As he looked at his reflection he saw a magnificent brown bear staring back at him.

"'The bargain is kept,' said the bear queen, 'but not in the way you thought. Now you will be my king, and together we will keep the creatures safe from Man.'

"Fat Foot grinned a bearish grin, and together they walked onto the surface of the Moon Pool and danced on the moonlight until the moonbeams rippled.

"From that day onwards, although Man still burned the trees and poisoned the land, She-Who-Dances-The-Moonlight and her husband Fat Foot made a safe place in the deep forests for all the creatures of the earth, and their children. In time to come their children's children told this story to the Bear Woman, the maker of magical tales who lives in a cave on a mountain top. And as *she* tells it, once every year, from the time of the grey twilight to the return of the rising sun, the Children of the Bear join hands together and sing and dance and drum on the earth, so that no one who hears their tale shall ever forget the bravery of the bear king Fat Foot, and his beautiful bear queen."

The Rabbit's Story

Adèle Geras

"Stop snarling, Wolf," scolded an elephant. "You're frightening the bunnies."

"I'm not scared!" said a little grey rabbit. "You don't know how brave rabbits can be. Just listen to my story!"

"You should never judge a creature by appearances," the rabbit began. "I know what you think when you see me. I am a white female rabbit: a doe, with long pink-lined ears and lovely pink eyes. I look gentle. I look mild. I look as though I would never hurt anyone. Well, all of that is true for most of the time, but once I became fierce. Once, I behaved as wildly as any wildcat, and as bravely as the bravest of lions. I bit a person. Hard, and without once thinking of the danger to myself. I'll tell you what happened, and you can decide how fluffy and soft I really am.

"At the time of this adventure, I lived with two companions in a pleasant enclosure.

They, too, were does. One was black, with two pretty white-tipped ears, and we called her Daisy. The other was brown and tiny and we called her Bonnie. My name is Snow, because of my perfectly white fur.

"The people who looked after us were kind, and fed us well with leaves and also with whatever was left from the vegetables they put on their own tables. So it was that we grew to love carrots and turnips and especially lettuce with its deliciously frilly leaves. We would have spent our whole lives like this, in great contentment, but then something dreadful happened. The rain stopped falling from the sky, and the earth dried up and we never saw a green leaf from one day to the next. At first, the people shared what they had with us, but one black day the sun travelled right across the sky and the darkness fell and no one came to give us food. We soon discovered that the humans had gone.

"'They're looking for something to eat,' said Bonnie. 'Maybe when they find it, they'll come back and share it with us.'

"'I don't think we should wait here, though,' said Daisy. 'Let's bite our way out and go and find some food for ourselves.'

"'We'll go tomorrow,' I agreed. 'Let's sleep now. We'll need all our energy to bite through this fence in the morning.'

"We slept. I woke suddenly, my nose twitching and quivering. Someone or something whose smell I didn't recognise was near our enclosure. I looked around and then I saw him: a man. Not one of our humans, or one of our humans' neighbours. A stranger. I could tell at once that he meant us no good at all. He opened the gate, and went up to the covered part of our home. Bonnie and Daisy were awake by now too, of course. Rabbits wake up at the slightest noise. They were terrified, and trembling all over. The man said:

"'Ah, my beauties, what a fine rabbit stew you will make for me and my children.'

"He picked Daisy and Bonnie up by their ears, and held them in the air.

"'Help!' they both squeaked. 'Snow! Snow! Do something … help us! We don't want to be a fine stew … please, help us!'

"To this day, I don't know where I found the courage. Anger filled me, and made my ears stand up stiffly. It made me forget that I was a small, fluffy rabbit and for a few moments I imagined I was the strongest and cruellest creature that had ever walked the earth. I threw myself at the man's leg, and clamped my teeth … my hard, white, wood-chomping teeth … into the plump flesh just above his ankle.

"'Owwww!' he cried, and in his pain he dropped Daisy and Bonnie on the ground.

"'Quick!' I shouted. 'He's left the gate open … let's go. Come on, follow me.'

"We ran until our enclosure was left far behind us. And as we ran, we could hear the howls of the bitten man carrying through the quiet night air. We stopped running when we came to the oak tree.

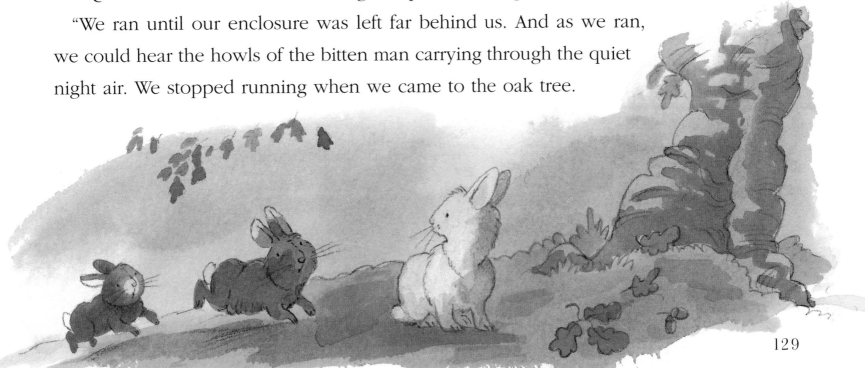

"'How brave you were!'
Bonnie said.

"'If it wasn't for you,' said Daisy,
'we would be skinned and cut up,
ready for the pot.'

"We all shivered with terror. I said:

"'Any rabbit would have done the same. It was an emergency.'

"When we woke up in the morning we set off to look for something to eat, and just over the hill we found a vegetable garden with a few things still growing in it. We were very lucky rabbits, and I am the luckiest of all because I am here to tell you this story. I hope my two friends, wherever they are, are safe and happy."

The Camel's Story

Vivian French

"WRRR!!!" "SPIT!" "BANG!" "WRRRRR!"

Noah sighed.

"Is that the camels?" he asked.

Mrs Noah nodded.

"I don't know what's wrong with them," she said. "They've been nothing but trouble ever since they came on board. Argue, argue, argue. They never stop!"

"Funny looking things, camels," Ham said thoughtfully. "No one ever told me they had humpy things on their back."

"Now you come to mention it," Noah said, "I think the humps ARE new. I'm almost sure they didn't have them there last year."

There was another loud crash, and a "W'RRRRR!!" and a "SPITTTT!!"

131

"There they go again," said Mrs Noah. "Whatever can we do?"

"Hey!" Shem snapped his fingers. "I know! Why don't we ask them to tell us a story?" He winked at Ham. "And maybe we'll find out what they're arguing about."

Ham pushed him.

"You're just nosy."

"Yes," said Shem. "And you're a know-it-all!"

"Boys, boys!" said Mrs Noah. "You're as bad as the camels!"

"Ham," said Noah, "go and get the camels. And you go with him, Shem. And NO ARGUING ON THE WAY!"

Ham came back with Mr Camel. Mrs Camel, flouncing a little, followed behind with Shem.

"My dear camels," said Noah, "we wondered if you would be good enough to tell us a story?"

"HA!" said Mrs Camel. "I'll tell you a story, all right! I'll tell you a story about a BIG mistake!"

Mr Camel sniffed.

"ANYONE can make a mistake. Only YOU would make such a fuss about it. Fuss, fuss, fuss – that's all you do!"

"Now, now," said Noah, in his most soothing voice. "Why don't we have a story, and all calm down. I'm sure the mistake – whatever it was – can't be that bad."

"That's exactly right, Mr Noah," said Mr Camel, and he folded up his long legs and sat down.

"HO! YES IT IS!" Mrs Camel flumped down onto the deck, as far away from Mr Camel as she could. "Just you listen!"

"In the beginning, when God made the animals, he made us camels look TERRIBLY ordinary. In fact, God made most of the animals more or less the same. You know the sort of thing. A blob of clay for the body. Four little blobs for the legs. Another blob for the head. A couple of shiny stones for the eyes, and there you are. Instant animal. No skill needed."

Mrs Camel paused, and gave the hippopotamuses a sneery look.

"Some of us haven't changed one bit, if you ask me. Anyway, there we were. We had short legs, and short necks, and looked ORDINARY." Mrs Camel sniffed. "Of course we knew we deserved MUCH better than that. I mean, we were CAMELS! We went to see God, but he was too busy making men and women to be bothered with us. So – we decided that we would take ourselves off. We would live as far away from those dreadfully boring hippos and cats and bears and lions as we could go.

"So we walked … and we walked and we walked and we walked. We walked so far that our feet grew quite flat, and our legs grew long. Of course, from time to time we met a zebra or a wombat or a tiger, but we just looked over their heads. They soon learnt not to bother us. And our necks grew longer and longer, until we looked rather wonderful – even if I do say so myself."

"So, THAT'S why they've got such a snooty look!" Shem whispered to Ham.

"Sh!" said Noah.

Mrs Camel took no notice of the interruption.

"At last we found a SPLENDID place to live. It was right up at the top of a mountain, far FAR away from those nasty common animals. No one EVER bothered us – not even those horrid human beings."

Mrs Camel caught Noah's eye.

"Oh, I DO beg your pardon, Noah – I don't mean present company, of course!"

Noah nodded, and Mrs Camel went on.

"Anyway, there we were. No bother to anyone, and no one bothering us – except for God, and we didn't really mind that. We showed him our beautiful long legs and our delightfully flat feet and our splendidly long necks, and he said 'Fine, fine – if that's what you want, I'll make sure camels always look like that.' He was no trouble. He liked to sit on the top of our mountain and watch what was going on in the world below."

Mrs Camel stopped for a moment, and glared at Mr Camel.

"And THAT'S when it all started. Mr Camel, Mr CLEVER CLOGS Camel, he began to chat to God. Thought he was God's best friend after a couple of days. By the end of the week he was telling God what he should and shouldn't do. By the end of a fortnight you'd have thought he'd made the world all by himself!"

Mr Camel coughed.

"Ahem. I did make a couple of quite useful suggestions, my dear."

"Oh, YES!" Mrs Camel nodded. "Like suggesting that fish should have flying lessons! And birds should swim! REALLY!"

"Some of them learnt all right," Mr Camel said, but Mrs Camel ignored him.

"So there Mr Camel was, laying down the law, when one day God dropped in looking cross. He said the humans were behaving TERRIBLY badly, and they were NOT looking after the world.

"'I'll keep the good people,' God said, 'but I'll get rid of the bad ones. But how? H'm … let me think. What about the sun? or maybe the rain? Forty days and forty nights should do it …'

"So what did Mr Know-it-all Camel say?

"He said, 'That's it, God! BINGO idea! Stop the rain! Blast them with forty days of sunshine!

Then everything will dry up, and there'll be nothing for those horrible people to eat, and they'll shrivel up and blow away. And good riddance to them! There. Problem solved. No – don't thank me – I'm always happy to help.'

"And Mr Camel was so pleased with himself he never even waited to see what God thought of his idea. He came RUSHING down the path to where we were nibbling twigs.

"'Whatever's up?' we asked.

"'Listen! It's our BIG chance!' he said. 'If we can learn how to do without water for forty days and forty nights we can be THE ONLY ANIMALS LEFT! Men, women, tigers, wombats, elephants – they'll all shrivel up and blow away! It'll just be us – us and God. Oh, and a few good people, IF God can find any, which I doubt!'

"So there we were. We learnt to go without water for one week, and then two. Then three weeks. At last we could do it … we didn't need to drink for forty days and forty nights.

"The next time God dropped in for a chat Mr Camel said, 'So, God – when's the rain stopping?'

"'WHAT?' said God.

"Mr Camel said, 'When's the rain stopping? When are you going to dry up the world?'

"Then God said, 'But Camel – I'm not going to DRY up the world – I'm going to send a FLOOD!' And he gave Mr Camel a very sideways look, and he said, 'So THAT'S why you've been trying to live for forty days and forty nights without water! I SEE! But I'm not at all sure I like the idea of you trying to be one better than the other animals. H'm. Let me think.' And God rubbed his ear. 'Yes. I'm going to teach you a lesson. When the flood dies down again you won't live on a mountain. Oh, no. You wanted DRY, so I'll give you DRY. You'll live in the sandy desert, where it's as flat as your feet. And just in case you forget WHY you're living in the desert I'll give you your very own mountain on your back … for ever and ever and EVER!'"

Mrs Camel stopped, and let out a LOUD snort.

"So THAT'S why we've got these HUMPS on our backs! And why we WON'T be living on our mountain. And why we WILL have to mix with all the other animals. And WHOSE fault is it? Mr Camel's!"

Noah stroked his beard.

"Well," he said. "I think your humps are rather splendid. And if you're living in a desert, you won't have to climb up and down, will you? And I'm sure you won't be bothered too much with other animals. I mean – who else can go for forty days and forty nights without water?"

Mrs Camel and Mr Camel looked at Noah. Then they looked at each other.

"Oh," said Mrs Camel.

"Aha!" said Mr Camel.

And they walked away together without a word of argument … looking over the heads of all the other animals as they went.

The Kingfisher's Story

Lucy Coats

"Let's have something peaceful and soothing, please, after all that excitement with the camels," said Noah. "What about the kingfishers? Two beautiful birds like yourselves must have a wonderful story to tell. How did you come by your feathers?"

One of the kingfishers stepped forward, puffed out her chest and took a deep breath.

"It's an old, old story," she began.

"In the far away and long ago times when mysterious beasts walked the earth, there lived a little brown bird called Fisher, with his little brown wife. They had a little brown nest in a little brown bank, by the side of a deep brown river filled with sparkling jewel-fish.

"Mrs Fisher was a happy little bird, but her husband was always complaining.

"'It's not fair!' he would say. 'I'm the cleverest of all the fishing birds, so I should be the king.

But I haven't got a royal crown and as for my feathers – well, just look at them. How can a king wear a cloak of this colour?'

"Mrs Fisher looked at him.

"'Your feathers are a very nice brown, dear,' she replied. 'They go with the nest walls.'

"But Fisher complained and complained, until one day Mrs Fisher got fed up.

"'If you're so unhappy, dear,' she said, 'why don't you ask Water Dragon to help you? My old mother said he lives at the bottom of the Great Lake by the Big River.'

"So Fisher caught up some of the prettiest jewel-fish for a present, and set off to find Water Dragon. He flew till his little wings ached, and at last he saw the Great Lake by the Big River. He plunged in, and flew down and down till he reached a cave at the very bottom. And there, all curled up, was a very small dragon, covered in beautiful rainbow scales.

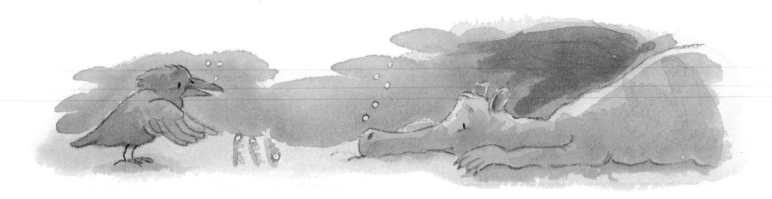

"'Oh mighty Water Dragon,' said Fisher. 'I want to be a king with a royal crown and a royal cloak. Can you help me?' And he laid the jewel-fish by the dragon's nose.

"A long, long tongue snaked out, and the fish were gone in a gulp.

"'Very nice!' said the dragon, sleepily. 'But my power is weak today. Go and see my sister, Earth Dragon. She lives under Draco Mountain.'

"So Fisher picked a bunch of golden kingcups from the lakeside as a present, and flew off to Draco Mountain.

"Soon he found a cave entrance. It was very dark, and he kept bumping into things, but at last he saw a glow of light at the end of a long passage.

"Stretched out on a grassy hill, and covered in spring flowers, lay Earth Dragon. She was very large and very beautiful, and Fisher laid his bunch of kingcups in front of her and bowed.

"'Oh mighty Earth Dragon,' he began. 'I want to be a king with a royal crown and a royal cloak. Can you help me?'

"Earth Dragon sniffed the kingcups and sighed.

"'How pretty!' she said. 'But I can't help you today, because I am making the earth beautiful for springtime. Why don't you try my sister, Air Dragon? She lives in a cloud above the Cave of the Winds.'

"Fisher was very tired, and he didn't know where the Cave of the Winds was, so he flew back to his wife. How pleased she was to see him.

"But Fisher was still unhappy. He had no royal crown and no royal cloak. So Mrs Fisher knitted him a beautiful scarf of river mist as a present for Air Dragon, and sent him off again.

"'The Cave of the Winds is to the north,' she said. 'Or so my old mother always told me.'

"Fisher flew northwards until his little wings were heavy with ice. The winds blew him about in every direction, but at last he landed on the ledge of a huge cave. Above it hung a pink cloud. Sitting on top of the cloud was an enormous crystal dragon. Fisher laid his scarf of mist by her glittering tail, and bowed deeply.

"'Mighty Air Dragon,' he whispered. 'I want to be a king with a royal crown and a royal cloak. Can you help me?'

"Air Dragon twitched the scarf around her neck with a flick of her tail.

"'It's my day off,' she snorted. 'Go and see my brother, Fire Dragon. I always send wish-wanters to him. You'll find him at the top of the last volcano between the Sun and the Moon.'

"Poor Fisher collected some river-gold as a present for Fire Dragon, and then he set off again. It was a long, weary way to the top of the last volcano between the Sun and the Moon, and it was very hot when he got there. The giant Fire Dragon lay curled around a blazing pile of jewels and treasure. Fisher carefully laid down his little bag of river-gold by the dragon's right paw.

"'Mighty Fire Dragon,' he began. But the dragon interrupted.

"'My brothers and sisters have told me of your wish, little Fisher,' he growled. 'But first you must show us that you are really brave enough to be the king of all the fisher birds. You must fly to the heart of the volcano, and bring back a fire jewel. Only then will we grant you your royal crown and your royal cloak.'

"Fisher shivered as he looked down at the fiery depths of the volcano. But he truly wanted to be a king, so he opened his wings and plunged downwards. Oh! How hot it was! How his feathers burned!

"At the very bottom he seized a fire jewel in his beak. It hissed and smoked as he shot upwards and laid it at Fire Dragon's feet.

"Fire Dragon took the fire jewel and stroked it down Fisher's back. All Fisher's dull brown feathers dropped away, and in their place appeared a feathered cloak the colour of shimmering azure water, a crown speckled with flower blue and rich earth-brown, and a waistcoat of white ice-mist and orange fire.

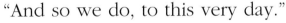

"'We name you Kingfisher,' roared four earthy, airy, fiery, watery dragony voices. 'May you rule over the fisher birds forever.'

"And so we do, to this very day."

The Guinea Pig's Story

Lucy Coats

"Who shall we hear from this evening?" Noah asked.

"What about them telling us a story?" said one of the animals, nodding at the guinea pigs.

"Yes, yes!" cried all the others. "It's their turn to tell a story!"

But the guinea pigs wouldn't. They were too shy! They put their paws in their mouths and tried to hide behind an elephant.

"Don't bully them," said the elephant. "They're only little."

"Everybody's got to tell a story!" The skunk thumped a foot. "Fair's fair!"

So the guinea pigs whispered their story to the elephant, and she told it for them.

"This is a rather sad story," she warned.

"Tell it, tell it!" cried the skunk.

"I want to hear!"

"Well, there was this evil king," began the elephant.

"What evil king? Who was he? What was his name? Be more precise!"

"I can't," said the elephant. "They don't know who he was. They don't know his name. Everyone just called him 'Your Majesty'. He was extremely cruel and everyone was frightened of him."

"Why?" said the skunk. "What did he do?"

"He tortured people. If anyone upset him, he would hang them upside down or stretch them on a rack or bury them alive. He would do it for all kinds of reasons. One time a poor serving wench spilt some soup on his new robes. Another time, a little boy kicked his ball into the palace gardens and it hit the king on the head. He boiled them both in oil."

The other animals looked absolutely horrified. The guinea pigs crept closer to the elephant.

"Naturally," said the elephant, "as you can imagine, the king made a lot of enemies. There were a great many people who would have liked to be rid of him. As a result, the king lived in terror that someone would poison him. And, indeed, a lot of people tried! But they never succeeded. This was because the king would never eat anything until it had been tried out on a guinea pig. Whenever a new dish was put before him, he would shout, 'Fetch me a guinea pig!'

"The guinea pigs were kept in cages, in the royal dungeons. Every time the cry went up, 'Fetch me a guinea pig!' the poor creatures shivered and shook. Because nine out of every ten dishes that the guinea pigs were forced to eat were poisoned, dish after dish was discarded, and guinea pig after guinea pig dropped down dead. The king was using up guinea pigs faster than he could breed them! In the end there were only two left."

The elephant wrapped her trunk protectively round the two little ones.

"The king was having a big banquet that night. There was bound to be a lot of poisoning going on. Their fate was sealed! And then, at the very last moment …"

"What?" cried the other animals. "What, what?"

"At the very last moment, one of Mr Noah's sons came to the royal palace and said that Mr Noah wanted a pair of guinea pigs to sail away with him on his Ark."

"And the king let him have them?" said the skunk.

"Yes, because Mr Shem – or was it Mr Japhet? – told the king that the earth was about to be flooded and the king flew into a panic and ordered his servants to build him a boat, immediately. Far too late, of course! But he didn't care about the guinea pigs any more. So you were saved, my darlings, weren't you?"

The guinea pigs nodded, shyly.

"And now you're safe, with the rest of us!"

One of the guinea pigs whispered something, urgently.

"No, no!" said the elephant, shocked. "No one is going to drown you. When they want to test if the waters have gone down they'll send out a dove. I heard Mrs Noah say so."

"Not a guinea pig?" said the guinea pig.

"Certainly not a guinea pig," said the elephant. "I give you my word!"

The Skunk's Story

Michael Lawrence

As the creatures settled into life on the Ark, it became apparent that there was a very unpleasant smell in the air. Two unpleasant smells actually, at opposite ends of the vessel. The source of one was a mystery, but the other came from a creature who skulked between the apple barrel and the water trough in the prow.

"What manner of beast are you that you give off such a terrible stench?" Noah enquired through a megaphone one evening. "I don't wish to be rude, but you do *know* you smell, I suppose?"

The creature raised his furry head and shook his bushy tail, and when he shook his tail the dreadful odour increased tenfold.

A mighty groan went up and all the animals covered their noses and snouts and whatnots with anything that came to hand or hoof or paw.

"Of course I know," the unfortunate fellow replied irritably. "I am a skunk. Smelling bad is what skunks do best. I stink, therefore I am. Now would you mind leaving me alone to smell in peace?"

"Certainly," said Noah. "The moment you've entertained us. Such a smelly beast must have a very interesting story. Carry on, Skunk!"

"I have no story," the skunk replied grumpily. "When I was very young my mother and father crossed a road without looking and got squashed by a passing cart. I didn't go out much after that, and when I did everyone shied away. I'd still be indoors today if the waters hadn't risen and obliged me to join you lot. Wish I hadn't bothered now. No one comes near me. Lonely life, a skunk's."

It wasn't much of a story, but the creatures were moved by it, and shuffled closer, trying to pretend that it wasn't *such* a bad smell he gave off.

But suddenly a voice rang out. "You need be alone no longer!"

All heads turned. All nostrils flared. Another skunk!!!

"I've been keeping my head down at the other end of the Ark," the newcomer confessed. "I knew that no one would like my smell."

"I do," the first skunk said. "You have a wonderful smell. The grandest smell that ever wafted my way."

"I could say the same for you," the second skunk said shyly.

And while the other animals excused themselves with haste, the two smelly beasts parked their noses one against the other, and with quivering nostrils soaked up the sweet, sweet aroma of skunk in love.

The Jackdaw's Story

Jenny Nimmo

"Listen, everyone!" said Noah cheerfully. "This jackdaw here says he's going to tell us a story about *kind* human beings for a change! I'm going to like this story!"

"I was born under the roof of an old house in the forest," said the jackdaw. "Jackdaws like to live near humans. Their fires keep us warm in winter.

"There was an old woman and a beautiful girl in the house below. The old woman was always shouting at the girl. It kept us awake.

"I was the smallest in the family and my brothers and sisters were always pushing and shoving me. We grew and grew until the nest became too small for six fat jackdaw babies. That's when the others pushed me out.

"'Help!' I cried as I plummeted to earth. I couldn't fly and I had hardly any feathers. I landed in a rose bush so I wasn't hurt but I was very frightened. I thought I was going to die.

"The girl heard my shouting. She rushed and plucked me out of the bush, then she put me in her basket and took me inside. First she gave me water dripped from her finger-tips, and then she found insects in the garden and fed them to me. But when she heard the old woman shouting, the girl carried me outside and hid me in a hollow tree.

"Every day the girl came and fed me. Soon I had shiny black wing feathers and a hood of smoky grey down. The girl took me into the forest and helped me to fly. I would take off from her wrist, fly a little way and then come back and settle on her head.

"It was on such a day that our new life began. We had only gone a little way when a young man came riding up on a snow white horse. The girl was very happy to see him. I sat on her head while they talked together, almost in whispers. All at once the old woman appeared, like a dark whirlwind. She was all grey, except for a little twig thing that hung from her neck and flashed gold in the sunbeams.

"She thrashed the white horse with her long thorny stick, and it screamed and bolted away, carrying its rider with it.

"The girl cried out and tried to follow, but the old woman caught her hand and dragged her back to the house. I pecked her nose and the bony fingers that clutched my dear friend, but the old woman wouldn't let go. She screeched and swung her stick at me.

"'Fly away, little jackdaw!' cried the girl, 'or she'll make a pie of you!'

"I flew up to the empty nest where I was born. My family had all flown away.

"That night I heard the girl weeping. I fluttered down and perched on her windowsill. When I called, very softly, the girl ran to the tiny window.

"'How can I help you?' I asked.

"The girl touched her neck. 'The key,' she said. 'The key to my door.' And she touched her neck again. I understood.

157

"I found an open window and heard the old woman snoring. I hopped into the dark room beyond and moonlight showed me what I wanted: a little gold twig lying on a table. I took the gold twig in my beak and carried it back to my friend. She kissed my head, then fitted the twig into a tiny hole in her door.

"The door opened and the girl crept out with me on her shoulder. We ran into the moonlit forest that creaked and whispered, and we heard distant hoofbeats coming our way. The trees shivered and the white horse appeared with its handsome rider. He caught the girl round the waist and, as he swung her up behind him, we heard the old woman screaming.

"The white horse took us on a long journey to the place where the young man lived. I stayed with them for a while, and it was good to see them so happy. Then one day, when we were in the garden, the girl looked sad for a moment, and said, 'You must leave us, little jackdaw. You must find a wife and lead a different life, for you are a bird and we are human.'

"I understood.

"I was sitting on her wrist and when she lifted it I said, 'Goodbye! I'll never forget you.'

"As I flew away I thought my heart would break, but it didn't. I found a wife and we have a good life. Every day I tell her my story and she never seems to tire of it."

The Tortoise's Story

Vivian French

"I'd like to tell you my story tonight," the tortoise said in his low slow voice. "Of course, you may think it's really a story about a butterfly."

The butterflies fluttered and giggled and waggled their antennae.

"Do tell, Tortoise," they said. "Do tell a story about us!"

"Very well," said the tortoise, and he began.

"It was a very hot sunny day in the jungle. Butterfly was fluttering about like she always does – flitter flutter, flitter flutter – when suddenly she stopped. She could see something strange in the long grass; something smooth and round. She settled on a twig and looked a little closer, and then she nodded her head.

"'Yes,' said Butterfly. 'I know what that is. It's smooth and round, and it's in a nest of grass. It's an egg.'

"Butterfly looked again.

"'H'm,' she said. 'It's a very BIG egg. It must be the biggest egg in the whole wide world! Yes, that's it! And it'll hatch out into a Queen Butterfly – the biggest butterfly in the whole wide world! And then we'll fly away together. I'll wait and watch and see.'

"Just then Frog came hopping out of his pond, h$_i$p^{p}y h$_o$^{p}p$_y$, h$_i$p^{p}y h$_o$^{p}p$_y$.

"'Hullo there, Butterfly,' he said. 'What have you got there?'

"'Oh, Frog!' said Butterfly. 'Do look! It's the biggest egg in the whole wide world, and it's going to hatch out into a butterfly!'

"Frog hopped over to the egg.

"'Jumping tadpoles!' he said. 'That IS big! But I'm sure if it's the biggest egg in the whole wide world then it must be a King Frog. When he hatches out he will be so big that he will hop and jump to the moon!'

"'No, NO!' said Butterfly. 'It's a butterfly!'

"'Well,' said Frog, 'let's wait and see!'

"Just then Monkey came swinging by, to and fro, to and fro.

"'Hi, Butterfly! Hi, Frog!' he called. 'What have you got there?'

"'Come and see!' said Frog. 'It's the biggest egg in the whole wide world, and it's going to hatch out into a frog!'

"Monkey swung across to the egg.

"'Twiddle my tail!' he said. 'That IS big! But I'm sure if it's the biggest egg in the whole wide world then it must be Lord Monkey. When he hatches out he will be so big he will swing to the sun and back again!'

"'No, NO!' said the Frog. 'It's a frog!'

"'No, NO!' said Butterfly. 'It's a butterfly!'

"'Well,' said Monkey, 'let's wait and watch and see.'

"Just then Snake came slithering by, slither and slip, slither and slip.

"'Good morning, Butterfly, Frog and Monkey,' she hissed. 'What have you got there?'

"'You'll never guess!' said Monkey. 'It's the biggest egg in the whole wide world, and it's going to hatch out into a monkey!'

"Snake slithered along to the egg.

"'Shed my skin!' she said. 'That IS big! But I'm sure if it's the biggest egg in the whole wide world then it must be the Emperor Snake. When he hatches out he will be so long he will stretch round the world and back again!'

"'No, NO!' said Monkey. 'It's a monkey!'

"'No, NO!' said Frog. 'It's a frog!'

"'No, NO!' said Butterfly. 'It's a butterfly!'

"'Well,' said Snake, 'let's watch and wait and see.'

"Just then Elephant came marching by, stomp, stamp, stomp, stamp.

"'Good day to you all!' he boomed. 'What have you got there?'

"'You may look if you wish,' said Snake. 'It's the biggest egg in the whole wide world, and it's going to hatch out into a snake!'

"'No it's NOT!' shouted Monkey, Frog and Butterfly. 'It's going to hatch out into a –'

"They all stopped.

"The egg had begun to move.

"It grew a scaly head at one end.

"It grew a scaly tail at the other end.

"It grew four scaly legs.

"'Hullo, Tortoise,' said Elephant.

"'Hullo, Elephant!' I said. 'I thought I heard you coming!'"

The Tiger's Story

Jean Ure

"Grrr! Grrr!" growled a tiger, swiping lazily at a passing fly.

"There you go again, Tiger," said Noah. "Always growling! Why don't you tell us a story instead?"

The tiger looked rather offended.

"What's wrong with a good growl?" she drawled. "But I'll tell you a story if you like."

And she began.

"Once upon a time there was a little tiger cub who lived at the edge of the forest with his mother.

"One morning the little tiger woke up in a very bad mood. A very cross sort of mood. When his mother tried to groom him he cried out, in a paddy, 'Stop it! That hurt!'

"'Nonsense,' said his mother. 'Just keep still!'

"But the little tiger wouldn't. He wriggled and kicked.

165

"'I don't want to be groomed! I want to go out and play!'

"'Dear me,' said his mother. 'What a bad mood you are in! Come and eat your breakfast.'

"But the little tiger didn't want any breakfast. He pushed at it, with his nose.

"'Don't want it! Don't like it!'

"'What are we going to do with you?' said his mother.

"The little tiger stamped his foot.

"'I want to go and play!'

"'In that case,' said his mother, 'you had better go. I don't want a bad-tempered tiger.'

"So the little tiger went running off, into the sunshine.

"'Aren't you going to kiss me goodbye?' cried his mother.

"'No!' said the little tiger.

"He was in such a bad mood!

"All morning long the little tiger frolicked in the sunshine. He met some other tiger cubs, and they played chasing games and biting games and hide and seek amongst the trees.

"And then the other tiger cubs said they had to go home, and the little tiger thought that perhaps he had better go home as well. He was beginning to feel bad about the way he had behaved. It was the first time he had ever gone off without kissing his mother goodbye. Suddenly, he very much wanted to be back with her, to nuzzle her and bury his head in her fur and tell her how much he loved her.

"The little tiger went skipping off through the grass. He was tired and he was hungry, and home was the place he wanted to be. But then – something terrible! He smelt the smell of humans …

"The little tiger crouched in the grass, his ears flat, his lips pulled back. Humans! There were humans at the edge of the forest. They were dragging something … something tangled up in a net.

"It was the little tiger's mother! The humans had come with their clubs and their sticks and were taking his mother away! The little tiger gave a yelp of fear. And oh, worse and worse! A human boy had crept up, unseen, unheard, and was peering at him through the grass.

"'Why are you crying, little tiger? Is that your mother my people have captured?'

"The little tiger was terrified. A human boy! Speaking to him!

"The little tiger turned and ran. He ran until he could run no more, deep into the heart of the forest.

"There he stayed for the rest of the day, hiding in the undergrowth, trembling and whimpering, too scared to move. Not until darkness fell did he come creeping out.

"The humans had gone – and so had his mother. The humans had come and taken her, and he would never see her again. And he had been so cross with her! He had been so nasty to her! He hadn't even kissed her goodbye …

"All night long, the little tiger crouched at the edge of the forest, crying for his mother. But his mother didn't come; and by and by the little tiger became exhausted and fell asleep.

"As the first rose-pink fingers of dawn stole into the sky, the figure of a tiger appeared on the horizon. It paused for a moment and glanced back, along the path it had come. In the distance, a human boy raised a hand in salute.

"'On your way, mother tiger!'

"And the tiger dipped her head, and went on her way.

"When the little tiger woke up and found his mother back by his side, he wept tears of joy.

"'The human boy set me free,' said his mother. 'Not all humans are bad.'

"That morning, the little tiger let his mother groom him and ate up his breakfast just as good as gold.

"'Don't you want to go out and play?' said his mother.

"At first, the little tiger didn't think that he wanted to, not this morning. But his mother said he might as well.

"'Your friends will be waiting for you. Only this time, little tiger, give me a kiss before you go!'

"The little tiger gave his mother the biggest kiss there ever was. Never again was he going to be rude and cross and nasty! And never ever was he going to go out to play without kissing her goodbye …"

The Slug's Story

Michael Lawrence

"Paws up any animal who's met the slugs," said Noah. There was silence.

"Just as I thought," said Noah. "Nobody's spotted either of them. Well, it's time you slugs introduced yourselves and gave us a story."

So the slugs slithered forward, and one of them began to speak.

"We slugs are humble creatures. We don't expect much of life, and we don't get it. We keep our heads down and mind our own business and never bother anyone. My favourite way of passing the day is sleeping. I'm very fond of sleeping. That's why I'm called Slugabed.

"Another thing I like doing is eating. Once I start eating I can't stop till I'm fit to burst. I never do burst, of course, or I wouldn't be here now, talking to you. As a matter of fact, I was having a little snack the day I discovered that there was more to life than being sluggish.

"It was a Wednesday, I recall. One of the hottest Wednesdays of the month. A perfect Wednesday to sleep through if I hadn't just come across this big fat juicy leaf and crawled onto it and started nibbling. I was still nibbling when the leaf slid into the river, carrying me with it. At first I was rather alarmed to find myself floating away from the bank, but as the leaf drifted further and further out I began to enjoy myself.

"'Hoi, everyone!' I cried. 'Look at Slugabed the sailor!'

"Silas the stickleback, who'd been doing some gardening down below, swam up to see what all the fuss was about.

"'You be careful, young Slugabed,' he said. 'What if you fell in? You'd drown. Slugs are *not* water creatures. Try and remember that.'

"I just laughed. The big fat juicy leaf sailed on.

"Adam the water beetle and Eve the dragonfly were having afternoon tea outside Eve's home in the reeds.

"'Hello, you two!' I shouted, and did a little dance to show what a good sailor I was.

"The little dance caused the big fat juicy leaf to wobble. The wobble sent ripples across the water. Adam and Eve's tea went flying. Their water biscuits plopped into the river.

"I steered the leaf away as far as I could.

"Some way along, on the bank, sat Mr Methuselah the bullfrog.

"'Look at me, Mr Methuselah!' I hollered.

"Mr Methuselah scowled.

"'Humpf! Young slugs should be seen and not heard. And given the choice I prefer not to *see* them either!'

"And he closed his eyes to prove it.

"Suddenly the big fat juicy leaf began to shiver and shake.

"'Out of the way!' bawled Nimrod the pond skater. 'I'm in training for the Riverbank Skating Championships! Wa-heeeey!'

"I clung to the leaf for dear life. But it rocked and rocked and rocked and …

"Over the side I went.

"Fortunately Silas the stickleback had decided he'd done enough gardening for one day, and was just off for a nice cool swim when he saw me splashing about in the water.

"'Oh, Slugabed, Slugabed,' he said, tugging me to the bank. 'Why don't you listen when you're told? Slugs and water don't mix, even on Wednesdays. Now stay on dry land where you belong, d'you hear?'

"'Yes, Silas,' I said. 'I will, Silas. I promise, Silas.'

"I sat on the riverbank. I was wet and slippery and not very happy. I gazed at the sparkling water and sighed. It wasn't fair. I wanted to be a sailor and it wasn't allowed. I'd have to stay on dry land for the rest of my days.

"Or so I thought.

"But then the Flood came, and the Ark, and here I am a sailor after all!

 Yaaaaaaaaaaaaaaaawn.

Excuse me. All this talking has made me rather weary. Slugabed the sailor must take a little nap.

Goodnight all!

Sweet dreams, everyone,

sweet dreamzz zzzzZZzzzzzzZZzzzzzzZZzzzzzzZZzzzzzzZZzzzzzzZZzzzzzzZZzzzzzzZZzz..."

The Pig's Story

Lucy Coats

"Quiet, everyone," said Noah. "This pig is kindly going to tell us a story. She's promised not to mention wolves, so stop prowling and growling, you two, and settle down."

The pig looked round nervously.

"It's all right," Noah reassured her.

So the pig began her story.

"Once upon a time there were five piglets called Thom, Indy, Middler, Ringaling and Smallest. They lived with their mother in a little cottage in the middle of a wood.

"Mrs Pig was rather lazy, and liked to lie in bed. She never did the shopping or the ironing or the cooking or the cleaning. Oh no! She made the piglets do it.

"'Well!' she said. 'What are children for, after all?'

"So, every morning she sent Thom off to the market to do the shopping. Indy stayed home to iron the shirts, Middler cooked the lunch, Ringaling swept the cottage, and Smallest squealed around under everyone's feet.

"One morning Smallest disappeared.

"'My baby!' cried Mrs Pig. 'Who will look for him?'

"'I can't look for him or I shall miss market!' said Thom.

"'I can't look for him or the shirts won't get ironed!' said Indy.

"'I can't look for him or the lunch won't get cooked!' said Middler.

"'I can't look for him or the house won't get swept!' said Ringaling.

"'Then I shall look for him myself!' said Mrs Pig. And she climbed out of bed, put on her bonnet and set off into the wood.

"'Grrrrh!' growled a wolf behind a tree.

"'Be off with you!' cried Mrs Pig, bashing him on the nose with her umbrella. And the wolf slunk off.

"'Next time I'll stick to little girls,' he muttered crossly.

"But that's not …" Wolf protested.

"Quiet now," said Noah, "and let Mrs Pig finish."

"Well, Mrs Pig searched for hours. She was cold, hungry and tired. At last she came to a sunny glade full of strawberries. There, fast asleep, was a pink piglet with a fat tummy.

"'SMALLEST!' shouted Mrs Pig thankfully.

"'MUMMY!' squealed Smallest.

"And when they had eaten every last strawberry together, Mrs Pig and Smallest ran squealing happily through the forest,

WEEWEEWEEWEEwee!

all the way home."

The Warthog's Story

Jeremy Strong

There had been two long days and nights of storm. The animals on board the Ark had become used to the ceaseless drum and hiss of the rain, but the storm was different. The wind churned the dark waters into raging whirlpools. The Ark was hurled and flung about like a leaf.

Many of the animals were sick and frightened. They lay on the dirty straw with their eyes rolling and their stomachs heaving, hardly daring to move in case they found themselves clattering helplessly across the deck.

One of the warthogs had been ill, but she was beginning to recover. She gazed at the desperate, scared creatures around her. She raised herself on her front trotters, until she was sitting upright.

178

"Come closer," she murmured, her voice hoarse from her recent sickness.

The other animals dragged themselves nearer, shuffling slowly across the deck, clinging to each other for support every time the mighty waves threatened to spin them round yet again. Another clap of thunder rattled across the black sky, but the warthog waited until everyone had gathered.

"I have loved listening to so many stories. Some have been funny, some exciting, some sad – so many different stories! But look at me and what do you see? Am I not one of the ugliest creatures to be found? I have warty, hairy skin. I have big tusks that poke from the sides of my mouth. I have a shunting, grunting snout for rooting about in the ground. My eyes are as small as grape pips." The warthog heaved a long sigh.

"As if being ugly were not enough, I am also quite hopeless at telling stories. It seems to me that what we need now, to take our minds off this terrible storm and lift our spirits, is a truly wonderful story." The warthog sighed again. "I simply do not have one. All I can do is sing. Whenever I have felt sad I have always sung to myself, and since I cannot tell you a story, I shall sing to you instead."

The warthog closed her eyes, and after a few moments of silence, she opened her narrow snout and a low, throbbing song began to spill from her squat, hairy body and, like some magic enchantment, it filled the whole Ark.

The warthog sang of the forest. She sang of the huge and ancient trees, with their leafy heads in the bright sky and their roots thrust deeply into the dark earth. She sang about the trees who listened to the secrets of the birds and the secrets of the worms and tiny creatures what lived beneath their bark. She sang of the dappled, dancing shadows that floated down through the layers of leaves until they rested on the forest floor, and her song was like a dappled shadow itself, floating and drifting into the souls of the animals on the Ark.

Then the warthog sang of the creatures of the forest, the chattering monkeys and leaping lemurs. She sang about gaudy parrots and flirting, flitting birds of paradise, with their feathers bright as a carnival, prancing through the branches, chasing each other across the skies, dashing and diving, swooping and swirling. She sang about the great snakes and the patterns on their skin that were like the rippling of sunlight on leaves, and her song was like sunlight within the hearts of the animals of the Ark.

Then the warthog sang of the great grasslands, where the wind sang too, and the big creatures moved like immense clouds across the surface of the earth. Elephants, buffalo, antelope, zebras, all of them moving with the green grass and the rain. She sang about the great feeding grounds and times of plenty, when stomachs became swollen with good living, and her song filled the animals of the Ark like good food.

And lastly the warthog sang of the high mountains, where the snow never melted and the air was thin. Yet even here there was such a bleak beauty that the iciest heart would melt to behold it. She sang of whiteness and jagged peaks, of crashing chasms and heaving valleys, and it seemed to the animals that the mountains were like a frozen storm at sea. And when the warthog sang of the mighty eagle, his huge wings fingering the air as he strode the crystal sky, the animals' spirits soared too.

When she finished there was silence for a long, long time. The animals hardly even noticed that the storm had calmed down, as if the warthog had soothed the very tempest itself. The elephant was the first to speak.

"You may well be ugly, Warthog," she said. "But you sing with the beauty of an angel."

The Bobcat's Story

Alan Durant

Next day, the animals woke up to a clear sky and a calm sea. They all felt much better.

"Let's have a story to make us laugh tonight," said Noah. "Who's going to tell us one?"

"I know a real funny story," drawled a bobcat. "Want to hear it?"

"Yes!" chorused the animals.

"One morning in the swamplands crawled a turtle, a little angry mother turtle.

"She came to a thicket of sawgrass where some cotton mice were playing hide-and-squeak.

"'Come and play with us,' they piped. 'You can hide and we'll squeak.'

"The little angry turtle shook her head.

'I've no time to stop and play,' she said. 'I'm going to the Alligator Hole.'

"'OH NO, NOT THE ALLIGATOR HOLE!' squeaked the mice.

"They were so scared-scared, they scampered away and hid in the tall grass.

"The little turtle crawled on.

"She came to a ferny glade where some young racoons were enjoying a picnic in the sun.

"'Hey, come and eat!' they called. 'We've got lots of tasty food to share.'

"The little angry turtle shook her head.

'I've no time to stop and eat,' she said, 'I'm going to the Alligator Hole.'

"'OH NO, NOT THE ALLIGATOR HOLE!' cried the racoons.

"They were so frightened-frightened, they left their picnic and vamoosed.

"The little turtle crawled on.

"She came to a little pond where some blue herons were busy fishing.

"'Come and fish,' they sang. 'It's hard work, but you'll get your share.'

"The little angry turtle shook her head.

'I've no time to stop and work,' she said. 'I'm going to the Alligator Hole.'

"'OH NO, NOT THE ALLIGATOR HOLE!' squawked the herons.

"They were so shaky-shaky, they hid their heads beneath their wings.

"The little turtle crawled on.

"She came to a custard-apple tree where a lazy bobcat lay, resting in the shade.

"'Hey, where are you going, man?' drawled the bobcat. 'Come into the shade and rest up a while.'

"The little angry turtle shook her head.

'I've no time to stop and rest,' she said. 'I'm going to the Alligator Hole.'

"'THE ALLIGATOR HOLE!' shrieked the bobcat. His whiskers quivered and his pointy ears stood up high.

"'You can't go there, man. That mean old 'gator will eat you alive, shell and all.'

"'Well, I'm going.' said the little angry turtle. 'And that's that.'

"'You're crazy,' said the bobcat and he shivered in the shade of the custard-apple tree.

"The little turtle crawled on … and on … and on … until, at last, she came to the Alligator Hole.

"'Hey, you, 'gator!' cried the little angry mother turtle. 'Come out, I've got something to say to you!'

"Then out of that black-black muddy hole came the biggest, meanest, snappiest alligator you ever did see!

"'Did someone call?' he growled.

"He opened his mouth wide-wide and his teeth were big and sharp as butchers' knives.

"The little angry turtle shrank back inside her shell.

"'Hey, what's up, little squirt?' roared the alligator. 'Has a snake got your tongue?'

"And he laughed and laughed at the little turtle, all in her shell.

"Then the little turtle got real-real angry all over again. She drew herself up and she thrust out her neck as far as it would go. And she said, very loud, as loud-loud as a little angry turtle could,

'YOU, MEAN OLD 'GATOR, GIVE ME BACK MY EGG!'

"Then out of the reeds and the grass and the trees, sudden as spirits, came the cotton mice, the young racoons, the blue herons and the lazy bobcat.

"'YES, YOU BULLY 'GATOR!' they shouted. 'GIVE HER BACK HER EGG!'

"The alligator looked at the cotton mice and the young racoons, the blue herons and the lazy bobcat. He looked at the little angry mother turtle.

"'Oh, hey, guys,' he grunted. 'It was only a bit of fun.'

"And he gave the turtle back her egg.

"Then he vanished quick as sand down into his black-black hole.

"The little turtle mother hugged her egg. She wasn't angry any more.

"'Now, I *can* stop and work and eat and rest,' she said.

"'But first,' said the bobcat, 'let's have some fun!'

"And so the little mother turtle and her friends danced and sang in the swamplands so joyful-joyful until the sun went down and the night came on."

The Penguin's Story

Alan Durant

"I've got a story about an egg, too," said one of the Emperor Penguins the next night.

"Then tell it to us," said Noah.

So the Emperor Penguin began.

"Now," he began, "that little mother turtle went to a lot of trouble to get back her egg – and good for her. But that is nothing to the trouble we father penguins take in looking after our eggs. Let me tell you about the time my missus laid her first egg. It was in the middle of winter in the coldest, bleakest, windiest place on earth, Antarctica – that's a long ways from the swamplands, I can tell you! It makes me shiver just to say the word and I've lived there all my life! Anyway, my missus and I had found ourselves a little place in the snow, nice and private like, and settled down to wait for the big event.

"Well, by and by, it happened: my missus laid an egg! I was very excited, I can tell you – and so was my missus. We trumpeted with joy. There it was, our first egg, beautiful and white as the snow all about us.

"'Our very first egg,' my missus said proudly. Then she pecked me on the cheek.

"'Look after it well, dear. Make sure you keep it warm. I'm off to the sea to get some food. See you soon.' And with that, she waddled away across the snow, leaving me with the egg!

"Well, I didn't quite know what to think! But I knew that I'd have to get the egg off the snow if I was going to keep it warm. So I rested it on my feet, nestled under the fur on my tummy. I was comfortable enough – apart from the wind howling and flapping around me like a mad sea-bird. I stayed like that all day … and the next … and the one following. Day after day I stood, with that precious egg on my feet, sheltering it from the icy wind. Fortunately my feathers are very thick and I don't feel the cold much. Weeks passed – and there was still no sign of my missus.

"'Well, this is a bit of all right.' I said to myself, because I was getting a little fed up by now, I can tell you, and a little peckish too – well, I hadn't eaten for a month! Imagine that, a whole month without food! There's some here among us – mentioning no names – who can't go an hour without eating! What I needed was some company.

"Well, as luck would have it, at that moment a group of penguins came shuffling across the ice towards me and, as they drew closer, I could see that each of them was carrying an egg – just like me! It was a funny sight, I can tell you – even for a penguin!

"'Come and join us!' called the daddy penguins.

"Well, I needed no second invitation: I was over the ice in no time, waddling and trumpeting. In a great huddle we shuffled on, chattering as we went. At first, we moved very slowly – well, you try walking quickly with an egg on your feet! Mostly the ice was flat, but now and then we came to a slope – and that's when the real fun started.

"Now, as anyone knows, the best way to go down a slippery slope is to slide. So we hitched our eggs right up, wedging them safely under our tummies, then whee! down we slid. Most of us took great care to make sure our eggs didn't bump on the ice, but there were a few who didn't, I'm sorry to say, and their eggs ended up broken and ruined. Well, those careless penguins got an earful when their missus came back, I can tell you!

Anyway, at last the big day came. I heard a tap, tap from under my tummy – and looked down to see the egg starting to crack: my chick was hatching! I watched with delight as the shell splintered and broke and there was a little, fluffy chick! My first chick! (He looked just like me, too – everyone said so.) And all around me daddy penguins were greeting the arrival of their chicks. We made some noise, I can tell you! Louder than a herd of barking seals we were and that's the truth.

"Now, when I'd calmed down a little, I soon realised I had a problem. Not only did I have to keep this young chick of mine warm, I had to feed him – and there was no food for miles and miles around and no sign of my missus either! Well, it being my first chick, I was at a bit of a loss, I can tell you. Fortunately, the daddy penguin next to me was an old-timer: he'd just hatched his fifth chick and he knew just what to do.

"'You have to use your milk to feed your chick,' he said.

"'Milk!' I exclaimed. 'I don't have any milk!'

"Well, I thought the excitement of the egg-hatching had made his brain go funny.

"'Yes you do,' he laughed. 'We daddy penguins have a special pouch in our throats for making milk to feed our young 'uns. I'll show you.'

"And he did. And he was right. And it came as a big surprise to me, I can tell you.

"Now I don't suppose there are many dads here who have fed their babies with their own milk. Well, I did. For days and days. And just as I was starting to think that I could make no more, I heard a familiar call from across the ice – and there was my missus!

"Oh, what a reunion that was. It brings a smile to my face just remembering it. I was trumpeting and my missus was trumpeting and our little chick was whistling. They were the happiest sounds you ever heard.

"'I'll take over now with the baby, dear,' said my missus when we'd all finally quietened down. 'You go off and have some fun.'

"Well, I needed no second invitation, I can tell you! I was off like that, joining the stampede of daddy penguins headed for the sea – and the biggest, best, most well deserved meal of my life!"

The Worm's Story

Jean Ure

"Please, Noah," said a little worm. "I'm sure nobody thinks worms have anything to talk about, but I know a really good story. Can I tell it?"

"Of course you can," said Noah kindly.

So the worm began his story.

"I am but a humble worm. I live in the earth, in the dark and the damp. I slip and I slime, I slime and I slip. I am very humble.

"No one ever says, 'Oh the heroic worm!' No one ever calls me King of the earth. No one writes stories about me or says how magnificent I am. I am just a humble worm.

"Yet I, too, have had my moment of glory! Once when I was slipping and sliming my way through the earth I heard this sound overhead. A sort of drumming. I stopped and I listened.

"'What is that?' I said.

"A passing millipede gave me the answer.

"'That is the sound of horses' hooves. A great battle has been taking place between two rival princes, Prince Goodwin and Prince Enoch.'

"I had heard of Prince Goodwin and Prince Enoch. All of us dwellers beneath the earth had heard of them. They were the two great princes who ruled the land above us.

"I asked the millipede who was winning this great battle.

"'Alas,' he said, 'Prince Enoch.'

"I shivered when he told me this for I knew that Prince Enoch was a bad man. Unspeakably evil!

"'The sound that you hear,' said the millipede, 'is the sound of hooves flying over the earth, carrying Prince Goodwin to safety.'

"'He is fleeing?' I said.

"'Fleeing for his life. But hark!' The millipede raised one of his many legs. 'Do you hear?'

"I listened again, and this time I heard the drumming of a great many hooves.

"'That is Prince Enoch. He is coming in pursuit. I must be on my way!'

"The millipede scurried off to find a safe hiding place. Even we earth dwellers tremble when Prince Enoch rides overhead.

"I felt that I should do something to help poor Prince Goodwin. But I am only a humble worm! I slip and I slime. What could I do against the might of Prince Enoch and his men?

"And then I had an idea. There are vast numbers of us humble worms, slipping and sliming through the earth. If I were to call upon my fellow worms and ask for their support, then maybe together we could defeat the evil prince.

"So that is what I did. Worms came from all over! From far and wide, and wide and far,

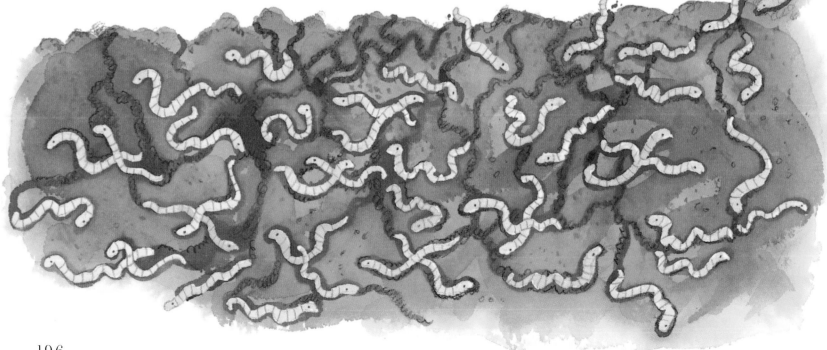

until there must have been a thousand or more of us gathered in that one spot beneath the earth. Then all together we slipped and we slimed just as hard as we could, so that when Prince Enoch and his men came drumming overhead, guess what?

The earth collapsed beneath them and they all fell in!

"In case you are worried, I will tell you that not a single horse was hurt. But Prince Enoch broke both his legs and all his ribs, and lots of men had very nasty bruises. Most important of all, Prince Goodwin was saved!

"I am but a humble worm, who lives in the earth, in the dark and the damp. I slip and I slime, and I slime and I slip. I am very humble. But I, too, have had my moment of glory!"

The Parrot's Story

Vivian French

One of the parrots was sulking. Noah had asked him (very politely) if he could be a little quieter.

"Squawk," said the parrot crossly.

"Why don't you tell Noah our story?" suggested his mate. "Tell him WHY parrots have got such loud voices. It might make you feel better."

"I suppose so," said the parrot. "All right, then, I will."

"A while ago," Parrot began, "all of us birds lived happily together in among the trees. We chirped and tweeted and sang our songs –"

"And SQUAWKED," said Mrs Monkey.

Parrot shook his head.

"No one squawked," he said. "Not then. We all sang and tweeted and chirped together.

It was wonderful to hear, and human beings liked walking in among the trees to listen to us – not that we took a lot of notice of the humans. We let them get on with their lives, and they mostly left us alone too. One day, however, one day two humans were sitting under my tree. All of a sudden one called up, 'Hey! Bright guy! Which of you birdie things sings the loudest?'

"Now, you may think it odd, but none of us had ever thought about being the loudest, or sweetest, or best. We just sang. So I didn't answer. But the human went on shouting.

"'Bet you can't sing as well as those big white birdies that swim on the pond!'

"Then the other human joined in. 'Nah! It'll be those shiny black ones that flap about. Bet you those are the best!'

"And the first human shook my tree and yelled at me, 'Listen, bright guy! What about a competition? Get all your little feathery friends together, and we'll see who's loudest!'

"'That's right!' said the second one. 'And we'll give a prize!'

"'EH?' said the first. 'What's that?'

"Then they stopped shouting and whispered together, and laughed a lot. When they had finished they came back to my tree.

"'It's all settled,' they said. 'You be here tomorrow, on this tree. And you bring as many big birdies and little birdies with you as you can … and we'll see who's the loudest. And whoever wins will get a prize, a BIG prize!'

"Well, I'd never been in a competition before. Neither had any of the other birds. When I flew around and told them what the humans had said some of them were very excited. The swans and the crows and the ducks and the geese and the owls all said they'd come to the competition, but the blackbirds and the thrushes and the nightingales and the robins said they didn't want to.

'I don't trust those humans.' said the oldest thrush. 'They'll be up to something nasty, sure as eggs is eggs.'

"The next day we got up early. You never heard such a lot of trilling and fluting as went on that morning. Even the birds who didn't want to take part in the competition were excited. The humans arrived quite late, and they brought lots of other humans with them. They seemed very excited too. They had cooking pots with them, and they made fires under our trees. It smelt hot and smoky, and I wondered if the oldest thrush was right. Maybe the humans WERE planning something nasty.

"I was about to tell them that we didn't want to sing after all when King Swan came paddling up. He looked so grand even the noisiest humans were quiet.

"'Before we begin,' he said, 'I think we should see the prize.'

"'Here we are, Your Majesty,' said a big human. And he whistled loudly. At once two little humans came running up carrying a wonderful house made of shining golden wire. It had the most elegant front door, and inside were bowls of gold and silver.

"'Only the best for the winner! A golden palace to live in!' said the humans, and we leant out of our trees to see better. The palace did look very fine, gleaming in the sunshine … and living in a tree or on a lake suddenly seemed very ordinary.

"'Very good,' said King Swan, and I could see his eyes sparkling. 'Let the competition begin!'

"Well – the noise was amazing! And it went on … and on … and on … and on. King Swan tried so hard he lost his voice and couldn't sing at all. The crows sang until they could only croak. The ducks sang until they could only quack. The geese sang until they could only hiss. And the owls kept flying round and round calling out 'WHooooo WHoooooo WHooooooo is the winner?' And my voice suffered as well.

In fact, I might as well confess it became a little … er … squawky. Anyway, at the end of the day we were all worn out, and we began flopping onto the ground one by one, croaking and hissing and quacking.

"'Time to choose the prizewinner!' yelled the hairiest human, and he picked up the golden wired palace and swung it to and fro.

"'I declare that the winner is –'

"We stopped singing, and waited … holding our breath …

"'ALL OF YOU!' yelled the human, and EXACTLY at that moment I saw that the golden palace wasn't a palace at all. It was a CAGE – and I squawked and I squawked and I SQUAWKED – and all the birds fluttered and flapped away and away, and the humans chased after them shouting and yelling about their dinners – but they couldn't catch us. Not at all. So they went back to their villages, mumbling and grumbling as they went.

"The birds were very kind to me that night. The nightingales even sang me to sleep … but in the morning, when I woke up, I found that I couldn't sing. I could only squawk."

Parrot stopped and a tear rolled down his beak.

Mrs Monkey put out her paw and stroked him.

"Never mind, Parrot," she said. "You've got a WONDERFULLY loud voice – and when the Ark reaches land we'll be very glad of it. You can warn us whenever danger is near!"

"Squawk!" said Parrot, happily.

The Duck's Story

Adèle Geras

The ducks were quacking even louder than usual.

"What's the matter with you tonight?" said Noah. "Oh, I know – you want to tell us your story. Come on!"

A beautiful green drake quacked, flapped his wings, puffed out his feathers and waddled into the story circle.

"It was a bit of a surprise to me when I found out what I was. I am a duck. You might think that's obvious. I have webbed feet, and a beak, and though I say it myself, a really eye-catching and rather splendid set of feathers on my head in a nice bluey-green that you often find on mallards. That's what I am: a mallard. See, I even know the *kind* of duck I am, which is cleverer than it might seem because there are many different kinds in my family. My Muscovy cousins are bigger than me, and my Mandarin cousins are smaller. I think I'm just the right size.

"But I haven't always known that I was a duck. It took me some time, in fact, to find this out. Some of you are shaking your heads in amazement, but it's true. Here is a fact you may not know about us: when we first emerge from our eggs, we grow attached to the first creature we see. We follow it around, and imitate it and think that whatever-it-is is our mother. This doesn't happen very often, because duck mothers are kind and loving and stay near their eggs whenever they can. Sometimes, though, tragedies can occur… oh, yes indeed… and a very sad thing indeed happened to me. The egg that I was in rolled away from the others in the clutch my mother was hatching. Down the bank and into the reeds beside the river I rolled. At almost the same time, men came and began to dig up the earth, ready for something or other to be built, and my mother and her other eggs were moved by kind people to somewhere far, far away.

"Fortunately, I was almost ready to be born when this happened, and even more fortunately, a human family was sitting on the riverbank eating some food on the day that I peeked though the shell.

"'Look, Mum,' said the little boy. 'It's a dinosaur. They come out of their eggs just like that!'

"'It's not a dinosaur,' said the little girl. 'It's a dragon. Just like the ones in the story you told me.'

"'It's not a dragon, and it's not a dinosaur,' said the children's mother. 'I wonder where its mother is, and perhaps there are brothers and sisters.'

"I was out of the shell by this time. I looked at the little girl and she looked at me.

"'Mum,' I said to her. 'You're my mum.'

"'Listen,' she said to her brother. 'It's talking. It said quack! quack!'

"Why couldn't she understand what I was saying? I spoke again.

"'I didn't say quack,' I said. I said: 'you're my mum'.

"'Can we take him home?' the little boy said. 'We can feed him. And look after him.'

"And that's what happened. They picked me up and wrapped me in a cloth and took me to where they lived. They called it Home. I knew it was called that, because I listened.

I listened to every word the children said, and by listening I learned a great many things. I was even given a name of my own, and I was proud of that. My name was Dips. I spoke to the children all the time, and while they sometimes understood what I was saying (they were always quick to feed me when I told them I was hungry, for instance) they *did* mistake much of my conversation for quacks.

"For a long time, I lived in my own place, which was called Hut. There was grass I could work on, and a little pool for me to swim in, but what I really liked to do was come into Home and sit with my family. I had my special place in front of the fire, and my own dish, so that I could eat my meals at the same time as my mother. At bedtime, I listened to the stories, and it was only after the candles were blown out that I was taken back to Hut.

"This went on for quite a long time, and then the biggest human, a man called Father, said:

"'The trouble is, Dips thinks he's human.'

"I was shocked, I can tell you. If I wasn't human, what was I? I certainly wasn't a cat. There was one of those who shared Home with me, and although I was a little nervous of him … he was a big, soft, fluffy, sleepy, ginger creature, who hardly ever bothered to speak … I knew I didn't look like him.

"The dog who lived with us made quite different sounds from me, and also had no feathers, so I knew that I couldn't be a dog.

"I can guess what your next question will be: how could I possibly have thought that I was one of those huge two-legged, unfeathered humans, who have nothing at all bird-like about them? The answer is because I saw them the second I was born, and it's a kind of duck magic that makes us think we ARE whatever animal or bird we see first of all.

"I waited to hear what Father would say next. Perhaps, I thought, he'd say the word, tell me what I was, but all I heard was, 'They've said they'll take Dips at the farm beyond the river. We'll carry him there tomorrow.'

"I was very sad that night. I couldn't understand why Father wouldn't let me stay here at Home where I'd been so happy.

"The next day, we made the journey to the farm beyond the river. There was a wide, tree-shaded pool, and on the water birds were swimming and talking to one another, and I found that I could understand every word they were saying. The water looked so cool and green, that when Father set me down beside it, I ran into it happily.

"'Look,' said my mum, the little girl. 'Dips loves the water.'

"'Of course he does,' said Father. 'He's a duck. All ducks love water, and even though we'll miss him, he'll be happier here with the other ducks.'

"A duck! That's what I was … I swam up to a plump brown bird who looked to me to be both wise and kind. I thought I had better make quite sure.

"'Do I look like a duck to you?' I asked.

"'Certainly!' said the bird. 'Only I would call you a drake, because that's the name we give male ducks. I can tell you are a male because of your beautiful blue-green feathers. You are a very handsome mallard drake.'

"All the other birds who were swimming about on the water gathered round to meet me.

"'Welcome,' they said. 'Welcome to our home.'

"'Is this pond your home? It's not a bit like the Home I've been used to …'

"'It's a home for ducks and drakes. Also for swans and geese.'

"'But my mum! I'll miss my mum!'

"'Do you mean that human girl, up there on the bank? She'll be back … she'll come and visit you. Humans like to visit us. They throw crumbs of food into the water for us. They are our friends.'

"And that was how I learned that I was a duck. Another surprise awaited me: the plump brown bird who first welcomed me told me a story. It was a sad tale about how she had lost one of her eggs on the river bank when men came to dig and how she was taken away to this pond with all her children but one, and how she had wondered many times what had become of her missing duckling.

"'That's me!' I said. 'I know it's me. I'm your missing duckling!'

"I like a story with a happy ending, don't you? I found my duck mother, and my human mother came to see me almost every day. I know she wasn't *truly* my mother, but ducks and drakes never forget the first creature they lay eyes on …"

The Owl's Story

Lucy Coats

The rain had stopped

"Do you think we'll soon see land?" asked a swallow.

"Noah said he was going to send out a dove to search for it," said a peewit.

"We'll talk about it tomorrow," said Noah. "Meanwhile, I'd like to hear from the owls."

A big handsome owl hopped down to the deck. "I will tell you a story," he said.

"Far away and long ago, when the world was new and shiny, there lived an owl prince called Good. He had a sharp yellow beak, soft creamy brown feathers, and a lovely screeching hoot that echoed loudly though the evening woods.

"In those days, the world was ruled by Oberon, King of the Fairies. Now Oberon had a very beautiful daughter, called Olwen. Olwen loved to walk in the woods at night, singing to the moon, and catching the starlight in a little net. Good often saw her, and soon he had fallen in love with the fairy princess.

211

"'Too whit, too wooooe!' he hooted sadly to himself. 'How can an owl marry a fairy? What shall I dooooo?'

"Now although Olwen seemed to be a perfect fairy princess, she had a terrible secret. All fairies have wings, and can fly. But Olwen could not. Her wings were as big and sparkly as anybody else's, but however much she flapped them she never rose more than a finger's width off the ground. One evening, as Good swooped silently through the woods, he heard a sobbing sound coming from a glade. He landed quietly on a tree, and there he saw Olwen, lying on the ground and crying her eyes out. Good landed beside her and brushed away her tears with his soft wing.

"'Whatever is the matter, dear Princess?' he hooted. 'What can I dooo?'

"'It's my wings!' sniffed Olwen. 'They don't work, and t-t-tonight it is my turn to take the King's b-b-birthday present to the Fairy Palace in the Air, *and I can't fly –*'

"Now owls are very wise, and Good was clever as well as wise. Here was his chance to help Olwen, and show her his love. He shut his big round golden eyes and thought and thought, and soon he had a plan.

"'I will be your wings, Olwen!' he hooted. 'You must make me invisible, and climb on my back, and then I will fly you to the Fairy Palace in the Air to deliver the King's birthday presents. No one will ever know if you flap your own wings a bit!'

"Olwen was delighted. She ran back to her own little Rose Palace in the woods to fetch the King's present and mix up an invisibility potion, then she climbed onto Good's back and snuggled down into his feathers.

"'The potion won't last long,' she said. 'So I will only rub it on you just before we get there.'

"Olwen was light, but the King's present was rather heavy, and Good was tired by the time they reached the Fairy Palace in the Air. Just before they arrived, Olwen rubbed the invisibility potion onto his feathers, and Good felt himself disappear with a POP! Olwen flapped her wings frantically, and they managed to make a graceful landing.

"'Follow me!' whispered Olwen, 'and try not to bump into anyone!'

"The palace was magnificent. The walls were made of rainbows, the lights were raindrops, and the furniture was made of pink fluffy clouds. Olwen hurried though the corridors on her way to the Throne Room. A fanfare of fairy trumpets announced her arrival.

"'The Princess Olwen to present the King's Birthday Present!' called a fairy herald as she entered with Good close at her heels. King Oberon was sitting on his mother-of-pearl throne.

"'Aha!' he cried. 'My favourite daughter! And what have you brought me, my dear?'

Princess Olwen hugged her father and handed him the heavy parcel, all tied up with ribbons of mist.

"'I made it myself, Father,' she said.

"King Oberon jigged about with excitement.

"'I do love my birthday!' he cried, as he ripped off the wrapping. There, lying on a bed of green moss was a beautiful crystal ball, filled with starlight.

"'It's to light your way to bed, Father,' said Olwen, softly.

"Good loved her more than ever – she was so clever to make something so lovely.

King Oberon thought so too, for he hopped off his throne and danced around with his present.

"'Oh how pretty!' he said. But as he danced behind Olwen, he stepped on something soft.

"'Too whit toow-ouch!' said the something.

"'*WHAT IN AIR IS THAT?*' exclaimed the King.

"Olwen began to sob.

"'It's my wings!' she cried, and at that moment POP! Good became visible again. Soon Olwen and Good had told King Oberon the whole sad story.

"'You silly girl!' said her father. 'I was exactly the same when I was a fairy prince. All you need is some of my Magic Flying Ointment!'

"And he sent for some at once. Soon Olwen and Good and King Oberon were flying round the Throne Room, giggling.

"'Wheeeee!' yelled Olwen as she swung round a chandelier.

"When they were tired, the King ordered a huge birthday tea, of fairy cakes and jellies and ice-cream. Good had never eaten so much in all his life.

"'Now!' said King Oberon when they had finished. 'You must have a reward, young owl! Tell me what you want most of all in the world.'

"Good took a deep breath.

"'Your Majesty, I would like to marry the Princess Olwen!' he hooted bravely.

"The King looked at Olwen, who was smiling happily.

"'Oh!' she said. 'Yes please!'

"And so it was that the fairy princess Olwen married the owl prince Good, and they lived happily ever after in the little Rose Palace in the woods."

The Lovebird's Story

Alan Durant

"I have an announcement to make," said Noah. "The water is falling. Tomorrow I am sending a dove out to look for dry land. This may be our last night together on the Ark, and our very last story. Who will tell us a happy story to end with?"

Two little lovebirds fluttered down and perched on his shoulder.

"We know a happy story," said one of them. "It's our own."

"Then let us hear it," said Noah.

"On a tree in a wood lived a little lovebird. She had bright colourful feathers and the cutest little yellow beak. Everyone said she was the most beautiful little bird in the whole wood.

"'You're as pretty as a peacock,' they told her.

"With every day that passed, the little bird grew more beautiful. Then one day her mother said, 'Well, my little peacock, it's time you found a mate.'

"'Can I be your mate?' asked a young lovebird who loved the beautiful little bird very much. But the beautiful little bird shook her head.

"'I'm as pretty as a peacock and only a peacock will do for me,' she said.

"So she left her wood and her family and friends and flew off to find a peacock. Sadly, the young bird watched her go.

"The beautiful little lovebird came to a big field. There on a log was a bird with a pretty red breast, gobbling worms.

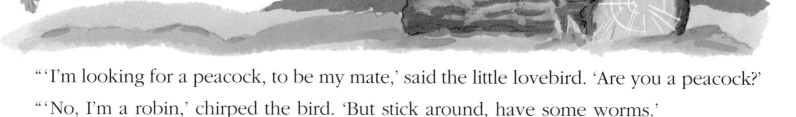

"'I'm looking for a peacock, to be my mate,' said the little lovebird. 'Are you a peacock?'

"'No, I'm a robin,' chirped the bird. 'But stick around, have some worms.'

"But the little lovebird shook her head. 'Only a peacock will do for me,' she said and away she flew.

"She came to some bushland. There was a snow-white bird with a splendid yellow crest.

"'I'm looking for a peacock, to be my mate,' she said. 'Are you a peacock?'

"'No, I'm a cockatoo,' squawked the bird. 'But hop up, make yourself at home.'

"But the little lovebird shook her head. 'Only a peacock will do for me,' she said and away she flew.

"On and on she flew until she came to a lake. There was a pink something in the water.

"'Hello,' called the little lovebird.

"The pink thing rose and rose into a tall, elegant, pink bird standing on one leg.

"'I'm looking for a peacock, to be my mate,' said the little lovebird. 'Are you a peacock?'

"'No dear, I'm a flamingo,' said the bird. 'But come on in, the water's lovely.'

"But the little lovebird shook her head.

"'Only a peacock will do for me,' she said and away she flew.

"All day, all night, she flew and she flew. She flew over a forest, where she saw a bird with feathers of all different colours, cracking nuts. But he wasn't a peacock, he was a macaw – and on she flew. *Would she never find the mate she sought?* The little lovebird wondered.

"Her wings were aching, her head was tired, but on she flew … until, at last, she came to a park. And there strutting proudly was a bird of the most beautiful blue and with the finest, longest tail she had ever seen.

The little bird's heart leapt.

"'I'm looking for a peacock to be my mate,' she cried. 'Are you a peacock?'

"The proud bird stopped still. It looked at the little bird with a beady eye. Then its tail opened out and Out and Out into a magnificent fan …

"'I am a peacock. See how beautiful I am!' it cried. 'Do you really think you're beautiful enough to be my mate?'

"Then it lifted its proud head and screeched with laughter.

"The little lovebird hung her head in shame. She felt suddenly very small and very, very foolish. She looked at the shrieking peacock and she thought of home, her family and friends, and the young bird who loved her.

"Then the little bird rose into the air and away she flew far from the park where the peacock screeched, over forests and lakes, fields and bushlands and back to the wood which was her home. And there sat the young bird, waiting for her.

"'Did you find your peacock?' he asked shyly.

"'Yes,' said the little lovebird. 'But I'm not a peacock, I'm a lovebird and a lovebird should be my mate.'

"She looked at the young bird.

"'Will you be my mate?' she asked humbly.

"The young bird could hardly contain his joy.

"'Of course!' he cried and he sang out loud."

And of all the pairs of creatures on Noah's Ark – the birds, the animals, the human beings – there is none happier or more in love than those two little lovebirds.

The lovebirds finished their story. There was silence on the Ark. The rain had stopped falling. The animals were all snuggled up together for the night.

Noah looked out at the water.

"Yes, tomorrow the dove can go out and look for dry land," he said to himself. "And soon the animals will be able to go back to their homes. I'll miss them. I'll miss hearing their stories. Pity we didn't have time for more."

And he went off to bed.

Funny, he didn't see the two little mice. And they didn't see each other till this very moment! They'd got separated before they came on to the Ark, and each little mouse had crept on board all by itself, hoping no one would notice it was all alone. They listened to all the stories, very quietly so no one would know they were there. Look back through the book and you'll see one little mouse hiding somewhere in the pictures for every story!